ALLERGIC TO BABIES,
BURGLARS, AND OTHER BUMPS
IN THE NIGHT

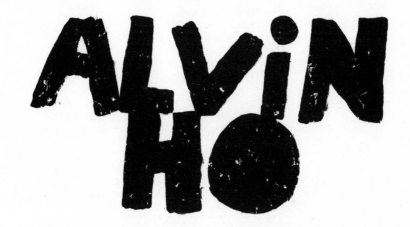

ALLERGIC TO BABIES, BURGLARS, AND OTHER BUMPS IN THE NIGHT

BY Lenore LOOK   PICTURES BY LeUyen Pham

schwartz & wade books · new york

Text copyright © 2013 by Lenore Look
Jacket art and interior illustrations copyright © 2013 by LeUyen Pham

All rights reserved. Published in the United States by Schwartz & Wade Books, an imprint of Random House Children's Books, a division of Random House, Inc., New York.

Schwartz & Wade Books and the colophon are trademarks of Random House, Inc.

Visit us on the Web! randomhouse.com/kids

Educators and librarians, for a variety of teaching tools, visit us at RHTeachersLibrarians.com

Library of Congress Cataloging-in-Publication Data
Look, Lenore.
Alvin Ho : allergic to babies, burglars, and other bumps in the night /
by Lenore Look ; pictures by LeUyen Pham.—1st ed.
p.   cm.
Summary: When fearful seven-year-old Alvin Ho learns that his mother is expecting a baby, he develops a sympathetic pregnancy—adding to his worry about the burglar who is targeting Concord, Massachusetts.
ISBN 978-0-375-87033-0 (hc) — ISBN 978-0-375-97033-7 (glb) —
ISBN 978-0-375-98889-9 (ebook)
[1. Fear—Fiction. 2. Pregnancy—Fiction. 3. Interpersonal relations—Fiction.
4. Schools—Fiction. 5. Chinese Americans—Fiction. 6. Concord (Mass.)—
Fiction.] I. Pham, LeUyen, ill. II. Title.
PZ7.L8682Akm 2013
[Fic]—dc23
2012011455

The text of this book is set in 14-point Adobe Caslon.
Book design by Rachael Cole

Printed in the United States of America

10 9 8 7 6 5 4 3 2 1

First Edition

This book belongs to
Sophie Fisher, who knows Alvin better than I do.
—L.L.

This one is for Cyrus Ahanin, who loves Alvin Ho.
—L.P.

AUTHOR'S ACKNOWLEDGMENTS

"Every child begins the world again."
—Henry David Thoreau, *Walden*

"Babies come from BabyStore.com, as everyone knows."
—Alvin

"It's the worst thing that's ever happened to me. He cries all night. He wears a diaper. He smells bad. And my mom and dad pet him like crazy."
—Scooter

"Babies need kissing."
—Anibelly

"It makes different cries for hunger, pain, fear, loneliness . . . and diaper change. And you have to figure out which cry means what, or else."
—Calvin

"Boys don't have babies, do they?"   —Nhia

"ICAN'TWAITFORTHISPREGNANCYTOBEOVER!"
                                                      —Alvin

MANY THANKS TO:

Ann Kelley for her incomparable editing.

The Phamtastic LeUyen Pham for bringing Alvin to life.

Anne Schwartz for loving Alvin even before he was born.

Lucy Dzina, who knows how to put on a hockey uniform.

Shepherd Dzina for wearing one.

CHAPTER ONE

A Dark and Stormy Night

it was a dark and stormy night.

My name is Alvin Ho. I was born scared and I'm still scared, so a dark and stormy night is a really crummy way to start a book.

CRAAAAAAAAAACK!!!!

BOOOM!

Usually it takes a couple of pages for things to get really creepy. But not this time!

CRAAAAAAAACK!!!!

Worse, I was already freaking out before the storm even began.

Normally, I'm afraid of many things.

Moldy food.

Hairy ice cream.

Hairy ears.

A full moon.

Battlefields.

Cemeteries.

CPR. (Cell phone radiation.)

Dark and stormy nights.

But this was not normal.

I had only one issue.

And it was DA BOMB.

MY MOM IS GOING TO HAVE A BABY!!!

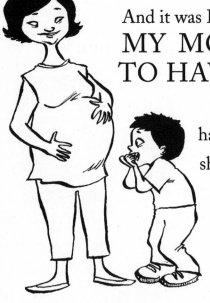

How this happened, I have no idea. My mom said she told us *months* ago, but I don't remember hearing about such a thing. Ever.

And now it's too late.

"Darling, you know I

can't return it," my mom said. "It's not the same as buying a toy and then changing your mind. There are no refunds on babies."

I knew that. Babies come from BabyStore.com, as everyone knows, and when your mom shops in the clearance bins you're stuck with whatever she buys. All sales final. No refunds. No returns.

The baby was a Final Sale.

I wiped my eyes on my sleeve.

It was after dinner and I was helping my mom put our dirty dishes in the dish-washer. Normally, I like helping her or my dad after dinner. It's our alone-time to-gether. Calvin and Anibelly aren't good cleaner-uppers, but I am, and so is my dad. But this was not normal. We were not alone.

Little ears were listening.

"Alvin," said my mom. "Don't you remember when we took your grandparents out for dim sum and your dad and I gave everyone the news together?"

No.

"Don't you remember that it was all we talked about at dinner for a while?" asked my mom.

Not really.

I thought we were playing the what-if game. You know, someone asks, "What if . . . Godzilla came to Concord, where would you go?" Or "What if . . . Babezilla were born into your family, what would you do?"

"There are pictures of the baby on the refrigerator," said my mom, pointing to the curling squares stuck to the door with magnets.

Baby?

That's a baby?

I thought they were satellite pictures of UFO landings!

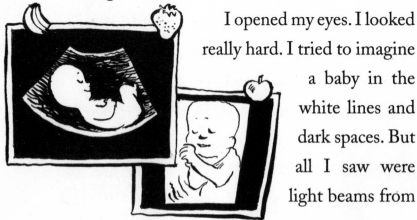

I opened my eyes. I looked really hard. I tried to imagine a baby in the white lines and dark spaces. But all I saw were light beams from an alien spacecraft, and maybe an alien or two if I concentrated as hard as I do for a spelling test.

"Alvin," said my mom. "Haven't you noticed the baby growing inside me?" She rubbed her tummy.

No.

I thought maybe my mom had gotten chubby, but I wasn't sure. Who could tell with all the loose clothing she's been wearing? I was pretty sure that one of the rules of being a gentleman is to *not* notice when a lady puts on a few extra pounds. But if you break that rule, then you'd better not even *think* of breaking the next one, which is to not ask her about it or else!

"Darling," said my mom, "I'm sorry you didn't know."

I was sorry too.

All I know is that my troubles began during show-and-tell, when Scooter showed pictures of his new baby brother.

"It's the worst thing that's ever happened to me," said Scooter.

"He cries all night. He wears a diaper. He smells bad. And my mom and dad pet him like crazy."

He wiped away a tear.

Then someone said that it looked like my mom was going to have a baby too.

It was news to me.

Then someone else asked when the baby was coming.

I had no idea.

"My mom says it looks like it could be any day now," said Flea, who's a girl, and who sits next to me. And girls, as everyone knows, are very annoying.

I wanted to set her straight, but I couldn't.

My voice doesn't work in school, where I haven't said a word since kindergarten.

"You should come over to my house and see the baby," Scooter said. "That way you can see the bomb before it hits you."

I nodded.

Then Miss P, our second-grade teacher, beamed and said, "Congratulations, Alvin! That's such wonderful news!"

It freaked me out! She's never congratulated me for anything, ever. And if it was such wonderful news, why did I suddenly feel so sick?

In fact, I ended up going to the nurse's office.

Soon after that, my mom had to come and take me home.

And I've been feeling like a ferry tipping to one side and taking on water ever since.

"Why don't you run along and relax," said my mom. "I'll finish in here."

Relax? How can anyone relax when they're on the brink of ruindom?

I mean, what if the baby's a *girl*?

I already have a girl for a sister, and the problem with a sister, as everyone knows, is that you can't thump her. With a brother, a good pounding usually settles everything.

Worse, how will I ever keep an eye on things? It's hard enough already with Anibelly getting into my toys, eating my food and drinking my chocolate milk.

Who can run along and relax?

"Is it a boy . . . or a girl?" I asked my mom.

My mom smiled her mysterious momsmile and rubbed her tummy. "I don't know," she said. "I want to be surprised."

Surprised???

"But I'm allergic to surprises," I said. "If a meteorite is heading for me, I'd like to know about it!"

My mom's smile disappeared.

Her eyes narrowed.

She crossed her arms.

The look on her face said she was NOT carrying a meteorite in her belly.

I blinked.

I wiped away a tear.

Then I ran into the living room and sat down next to Calvin, who was in front of the TV.

I breathed in.

I breathed out.

In.

Out.

In.

Out.

Extreme breathing is very loud, like my dad's car, Louise, when she's going uphill. It's something I learned to do from my scary *psycho*-therapist. She said to breathe deeply whenever I need to calm down, and to imagine my breath blowing away all my troubles like wind blowing away dust.

Cough. Cough.

It's never worked before.
And it wasn't working now.
I wasn't calm, or relaxed.
Worse, Calvin ignored
me completely!

CHAPTER TWO

The Rest of the Dark and Stormy Night

"calvin?" i said. "Did you know Mom's going to have a baby?"

"Of course," said Calvin, still not looking up from his phone. "Everyone knows."

"I didn't," I said.

"You're not so good at paying attention," said Calvin, his thumbs hopping up and down on his new cell phone which he got for no good reason except he goes to so many activities after school that he needs to

call my mom and dad for rides all the time, it isn't fair. He's nine, and I'm seven, which also isn't fair.

"But—" I began.

"Shhh," said Calvin.

"The recent rash of burglaries in Concord continued today with three break-ins before noon, and police say they may finally have a lead in the case," said the news announcer on TV.

Gasp!

"Stay tuned for more details."

I froze.

My dad was on a business trip in Connecticut, which is even harder to spell than Massachusetts. Usually, we don't miss him too much when he goes away for a few days. But this was not usual. It was a dark and stormy night. And there was a thief on the loose.

"Mommmm!" screamed Calvin, his thumbs hopping like crazy.

"You don't need to scream in the house," my mom yelled from the kitchen. "I can hear you just fine."

"Three more homes were broken into today," Calvin shouted.

"Oh dear," said my mom, hurrying into the living room. She sat down on the couch next to Anibelly, who immediately threw her arms around my mom. If I didn't mention Anibelly before it's on account of she's always hanging around me and Calvin but doing her own thing,

like a fungus between two toes. And my dad says it's not necessary to mention fungus, snot and earwax all the time.

"I'm scared," squeaked Anibelly, who's four and who's hardly ever afraid of anything. Not like me. I'm fearful of everything. Especially of Anibelly being scared.

"There's no need to be afraid," said my mom, pulling Anibelly close. "Lucy's a very good guard dog, aren't you, Lucy?"

"Oooowwwoooo!" howled Lucy.

"She said yes, right, Mom?" asked Calvin, his thumbs still bobbing like a couple of worms on the tiny keyboard.

"Darling," my mom said firmly, which doesn't mean "darling" at all when she says it that way. "You know the rules about the phone."

"I knnnow . . . ," said Calvin. His thumbs sped up, then stopped. "Sorry, Mom," he said.

My mom gave him The Eye. She likes us to be polite, and she's told Calvin a squillion times to hold his thumbs still while someone is talking to him.

If she only knew.

"Thieves think twice before coming near a house with a dog," my mom said. "It's just easier to go where no one's making so much noise."

"Did you hear that, Lucy?" Anibelly asked. She slipped off my mom's lap, slid down beside Lucy and gave her a squeeze.

I was this close to throwing myself at my mom and telling her how scared *I* was. But I didn't. I had a feeling a gentleman wouldn't throw himself like that at a lady, especially a pregnant lady. Worse, I was so freaked out that I couldn't speak—I couldn't even squeak—just like when I'm at school.

"*Concord police say a suspect was spotted leaving a house this afternoon on Jennie Dugan Road,*" the announcer said. "*The suspect was a white male, about six feet tall, dressed in a black coat, carrying a black bag and wearing black sunglasses.*"

CRAAAAAAAAAAACK!

BOOOOOOM!

"Police say residents should report any suspicious activity and lock their doors."

Music played. A shampoo commercial came on. A lady whipped her hair around in slow-mo, which made Anibelly get up and whip her hair in fast-mo. I was in no-mo.

"Lock their doors?" Calvin asked. "But we never lock our doors."

"We should take precautions," my mom said. She didn't sound particularly worried, which in a normal town might be okay. But we live in Concord, Massachusetts, which is hard to spell, and which is where the American Revolutionary War began with all sorts of explosions, and where famous dead authors are still in their homes leading tours.

BOOOOOM!

CRAAAAAASH!

Lucy's ears shot straight up.

Calvin jumped—which made me jump, on account of Calvin never jumps except to kick my butt. He knows karate, and someday he'll climb Mount Everest without oxygen, I just know it. And when you're tough like that, it takes a lot to make you jump.

"What's that?" Calvin asked, dropping his phone.

"It's just the wind," said my mom.

"It could be the robberer," said Anibelly.

"It's not the thief," said my mom, going to the window, but still not running to lock the doors. We hurried after her.

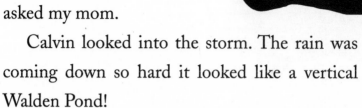

"How do you know?" Calvin asked.

"If you were a thief, would you be out tonight?" asked my mom.

Calvin looked into the storm. The rain was coming down so hard it looked like a vertical Walden Pond!

Thwap-thwap-thwap-thwap-thwap-thwap!
Anibelly covered her ears.

"It's only a branch hitting the house," said my mom. "There's nothing to worry about. When your dad's away, we've got *two* men of the house instead of one—right, boys?"

Thwap-thwap-thwap!

CRAAAAAAAAACK!

BOOOOOM!

Calvin and I looked at each other.

Then *ZZZZZAP!*

We weren't looking at each other anymore.

It was as black as a dead computer screen.

"Eeeeeeeeek!" cried Anibelly, followed by the sound of Anibelly being picked up.

"It's all right," said my mom in her let's-not-panic voice. "Let's find some flashlights. Hopefully, the power will come back soon."

"I'll get them, Mom," said Calvin, suddenly sounding like my dad. "I know where they are."

Calvin lit his way with the flashlight app on his phone, the bubble of light growing tinier and tinier until he was gone, like a shiny pearl swallowed by the vast black sea.

Now *I* was the only man of the house.

Thwap-dok-thwap-thwap-dok-thwap-dok!

I went skinless.

Waaaaaaaaaah! Crying is really great, especially when you're the man of the house and you don't have any scary quillery on your chin, not even a whisker.

Even the shadows on the wall were strange—my mom was as big as an SUV! I'd seen something like it before. . . .

This is the way it always happens on TV!

First, it's a dark and stormy night.

Second, it's a creepy little town.

Third, people are inside a house.

Fourth, shadows are stretching and dripping like wet swimsuits all over the place.

Fifth, things are knocking around outside like aliens have just landed and are about to kidnap you for human experiments.

Sixth, the lights go out.

Then FLASH!

Aliens are beaming you up!

"AAAAAAAAAAAAACK!" I cried, covering my eyes.

"Here," said an alien, beaming me with a light. "Take this."

It was Calvin. He thrust a flashlight into my hands and I clicked it on.

"AAAAAAAAAAAAAAAACK!" I zoomed upstairs as fast as my legs would go. I squeezed into my Firecracker Man outfit, then hurried back downstairs.

"AAAAAAAAAAAAAAAARRRRRRRR!" I
roared, racing at
face-peeling speeds
with Lucy by my side.

I LOCKED ALL
THE DOORS.

It was the most dangerous
mission Firecracker Man and Lucy
had ever been on! The Dynamite Duo
used to save the world every day, but now that I
have to save myself at school, my superhero
was a little out of practice.

And a lot out of breath.

Huff. Huff.

Puff. Puff.

Sput.

The floor pinwheeled be-
neath Firecracker Man. His
flashlight swung from his belt.

"Thank you, Alvin," said my mom, shining her
flashlight at me. "You're taking good care of us."

Alvin? Who's Alvin?

I puffed out my chest.

"I mean, thank you, Firecracker Man," said my mom, kissing the top of my helmet.

"Hooray for Firecracker Man!" said Anibelly, giving me a hug.

CRRAAAAAAAACK!

Lightning flipped the inside of our house eyeball white.

BOOOOOM!

Thunder grabbed the floor.

CRAAAAASH!

What was that?

Did something just leap past the window?

Was Firecracker Man the only one to see it?

"Grrrrrrrrrrr," growled Lucy. *"Grrrrrrrrrrrr."*

It was then that Firecracker Man got the bad, sinking feeling superheroes and dogs get when loved ones need to be protected and great danger lurks right outside their lair—that it was only the *beginning* of the most dangerous mission of his life.

CHAPTER THREE

Alvin Doesn't Look So Well

this is how you know winter has arrived.

You eat more.

You move less.

The heat hums in your house.

Your blankets are warm.

But the air is cold.

You don't *pop!* out of bed in the morning like you used to.

Worse, you can't even tell it's morning.

You could swear it was nighttime.

But if you did swear, your mom would have a few words for you.

And she's already saying hurry, it's time to go to school.

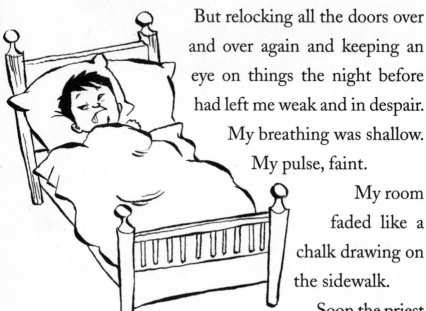

But relocking all the doors over and over again and keeping an eye on things the night before had left me weak and in despair. My breathing was shallow. My pulse, faint.

My room faded like a chalk drawing on the sidewalk.

Soon the priest will arrive to give me Last Rights, which is the last chance you get to raise your right hand and blink your right eye and bend your right knee. If everything works, you get a pass to go to heaven. Then you go.

Poor Alvin, everyone will say.

Poor me.

But it's the perfect way to avoid school!

Too bad death and school were in the hands of the nurses in charge, Lucy and Anibelly. And they were busy and bossy, as usual.

First I had to pass the Nurse Lucy inspection (easy).

Then I had to pass the Nurse Anibelly inspection (not so easy).

She put her ear to my chest.

She held a mirror to my nose.

"Mom!" yelled Anibelly. "Alvin's not dead . . . and he's not sick . . . but he's still in bed!"

I groaned a little.

I kept my eyes shut.

I rolled over.

"Oh dear," said my mom, coming into my room. She put her lips to my forehead. "Could this be Unfinished Homework Syndrome?"

I groaned again.

"Lost Report Card Disorder?"

I clutched my stomach and moaned.

"Hmmm," said my mom, turning me over and inspecting me like a bellied-up goldfish. "Groaning, moaning, shallow breathing, memory loss, lethargy, increased appetite, and enormous tummy growth."

I went limp in her arms, just in case.

"Urrrrrgh," I moaned, just for her.

"Strange," said my mom, giving my belly a rub. "Maybe you have a sympathetic pregnancy!"

A what?

I bolted up in bed.

My eyes popped out like bananas.

"It can be really rough," my mom said. "All of the suffering and none of the glory. But it's not a medical excuse for staying home. So rise and shine!"

My mom was particularly cheerful.

She gave me a hug.

She gave me a kiss.

Then she went to pack my lunch.

I ran to the mirror. I turned this way. Then I turned that way.

Eeeeek! I looked like I was in a fun house mirror!

Why hadn't I noticed a baby growing in me before? But there it was, as round and glowing as a *cha-siu-bau* in the oven. I couldn't believe my mom was sending me to school in *my* condition! If I was simply pathetic pregnant, shouldn't I stay home and *eat*?

Through my window I could see that Calvin was already at the bottom of our driveway waiting for the bus. He's always the first one there, and I'm always the last.

"HURRY, ALVIN!" my mom shouted from downstairs. "YOU'RE GOING TO MISS YOUR BUS!"

Hurry? How do you hurry when you're . . . gulp . . . pregnant?

I waddled out.

I grabbed a croissant in the kitchen and got

to the end of our driveway just as the bus pulled up and everyone rushed on. Everyone, that is, except me. I'm allergic to school. So I'm always the last one on. But today I nearly missed the bus altogether—I couldn't see my feet, or the step! In fact, I probably wouldn't have gotten on at all if it weren't for my mom watching me from her car in the driveway with Anibelly in her car seat waiting to go to day care.

"Bye, Alvin!" I read Anibelly's lips. She was smiling and waving wildly from the back. She's always so happy to see me come home, but she's also extremely happy to see me go. It's very strange. I can't figure it out. Girls are a mystery, my dad says. That's for sure.

And maybe boys are too.

I mean, HOW did I end up you-know-what???

I bit into my croissant.

I teetered like a bowling pin.

Then I tripped on the top step.

"Watch yourself there, sonny," said the driver.

"*Waaaaaaaaaaaaaaaah!*" I wailed down the aisle, clutching my PDK (Personal Disaster Kit), which was filled with all sorts of emergency equipment like floss, a bandana, a mirror, a scary mask, disaster plans and escape routes to help me survive school, but nothing to help me survive—gulp—a pregnancy.

The noise on the bus went round and round.

The money in my pockets went *clang, clang, clang.*

I could hardly walk. My pockets were heavier than my legs!

So I sat down. The only seat left, as usual, was the one next to Flea, which wouldn't be so bad if she weren't a girl. But she is. And the problem with girls, as everyone knows, is that they're not boys. They cry too much. They smell like cooked broccoli. Not like boys. We don't cry much—well, okay, I cry a

lot, but I don't cry like a girl, that's for sure. And we certainly don't smell like anything you could eat.

"That burglar was right outside our house last night," I heard someone say.

"He was at ours too," said Nhia. "But I scared him away with my ninja moves."

"You might have scared 'im away," said Sam. "But I nearly bagged 'im and hauled 'im to the cops."

"Well, I kicked his butt," said Eli, "and sent him flying."

The gang laughed nervously.

"How 'bout you, Alvin?" asked Pinky. "Did *Firecracker Man* scare him away?"

Pinky's the biggest boy in my class and the leader of the gang. He hardly ever speaks to me except to point out something embarrassing.

Normally, I would brag like crazy too. But I was not feeling normal.

I took another bite of croissant.

I sure wished I had some butter . . .

And jam . . .

Then I wished I had grabbed a second croissant!

"Look, he's still wearing his Firecracker Man costume!" said Pinky, pointing. "And the 'F' is for 'FAT'!"

Fat?

I looked. And sure enough, I'd forgotten to change from last night. And yup, my outfit was kind of . . . *tight* . . . around the middle.

I stuffed the rest of the croissant into my mouth.

GRRRRRRRRrrrrrrrrrr! went my belly again.

Flea's eye fixed on me.

If there's anything good about Flea it's this: She's a pirate. She has only one good eye and wears a patch over the eye that she lost in a sea battle in Boston Harbor. Also one of her legs is shorter than the other, which makes you wonder if it met with some misfortune at the jaws of a monster on one of those frightful expeditions off Nantucket. The problem is, she sees more out of her one good eye than most people see out of two. And the problem with sitting next to a pirate with a single eye who survived a whale attack on the high seas is that you might as well be sitting next to a surveillance camera.

And the problem with surveillance cameras is that they see *everything*.

"You were sick yesterday," said Flea. "And now you're sick again today. . . ."

Her eye was really roving now.

Worse, her brain was moving right along too. That's the problem with girl brains; they're plugged in and working all the time. Not like boy brains, which run on battery and need to shut down now and then to recharge and to preserve battery life.

"I've been watching you, Alvin Ho," Flea said. "And there's something not normal about you. . . ."

"I'm simply pathetic pregnant," I squeaked.

Flea's eye grew big and round.

"You're *pregnant?*" she asked.

The word hung.

The wind howled.

Everyone turned and stared.

"Alvin's *pregnant?*" Pinky shrieked. "But he's a boy!"

"Boys don't have babies," said Nhia. "Do they?"

The eyes of the gang looked back and forth.

My belly went up and down.

"Well, maybe it's a miracle!" Flea cried. "Like Christmas! Instead of the Virgin Birth, he's the . . . the . . . the Colossal Watermelon Birth!"

Oooh. I could hurt her. Seriously.

But I didn't. Flea takes Aggression for Girls, which has taught her a great many things, and me one thing: Don't hit a girl, even if she has only one good eye and one leg longer than the other and walks unevenly. Don't even think about it.

So I wished I could disappear. But I couldn't. I thrust my hands into my pockets instead.

Clang-clang-clang went all my coins.

My paper money went *chrrrr-sssssss-chrrrr*.

"Sounds like you used an ATM," said Pinky, suddenly impressed.

I was impressed too, but not with Pinky. He should know that ATMs only give out twenties— but I had emptied my entire jar of money that I'd been saving for a long time into my pockets right before leaving the house, which is much more remarkable.

Then Flea's mouth opened again—I didn't have to see it, I could *hear* it vacuuming all the air from in front of my face the way girls do when they have something to say.

"Do you think it's such a good idea to bring so much money to school?" Flea asked.

"You could lose it all," Sara Jane said.

"Or it could all fall out of your pocket on the playground," added Esha.

Oooh, girls are so annoying. Don't they ever listen? Don't they know what's going on?

"DON'T YOU KNOW THERE'S A ROB-
BER ON THE LOOSE?" I said. "IF I LEFT
MY MONEY AT HOME, IT COULD ALL
GET STOLEN!"

The eyes on the bus grew big and round.

The heads of the gang floated like alien space
ships.

Then, one by one, they exploded.

"OHNOISHUDDABROUGHTALLMY MONEYWITHMETOO!" Pinky screamed.

"MEETOOOO!" Scooter hollered.

"WHYDIDN'TITHINKOFTHAT???!!!" Sam cried.

Then the entire gang bawled like it was the end of the world.

Because it was.

When you don't know where your money is, then that's it for you. It's worse than being a watermelon in spandex.

CHAPTER FOUR

The Trouble with Eating for Two

the bad news about being pregnant is that there is always an announcement.

"Miss P, Alvin's pregnant!" Flea declared as soon as we walked into class. "It's a miracle!"

Miss P stopped.

She smiled.

"Actually, sympathetic pregnancies are very common," said

Miss P. "But they can also be really rough. It's a time of many changes for everyone in the family."

Miss P gave me a wink. "I had a sneaking suspicion about you yesterday," she said. "I hope you're feeling better today."

Then she looked at the gang.

"It's a good thing Alvin has you guys for support," Miss P said to them. "Maybe some of you have babies in your families and know what Alvin is going through."

I put on my run-over-by-a-truck face.

I stuck out my muffin-top belly.

Miss P's very nice, and there's always hope that she'll send me home.

But she didn't.

Instead, I had to get in line like everyone else and march to the library.

Normally, I like library hour. Our librarian will read something to us and then let us find a book to borrow. If you make too much noise, you can end up in the principal's office. If you're quiet, like me, you can get a free bookmark when you check out.

But this was not normal.

Clangclangclang! went all the money in my pockets.

Flea's one good eye followed me, stuck like a gumball to my hair.

Worse, Miss P now had her eyes on me too. Worser, she likely has a second pair of eyes in the back of her head, just like my mom. She guessed right away that I had my entire life savings in my pockets and said that maybe I should give it to her for safekeeping until it was time to go home.

"I'm just saying," said Miss P.

I kept my eyes down.

I clutched my PDK.

But the problem with having your entire life savings in your pockets in the library is that it's very noisy.

And the library is very quiet.

"Sounds like someone robbed a bank," said

the librarian as I walked past. "Don't try to hide from the police in my stacks."

Lucky for me, I had my PDK, so I put most of my money into it for safekeeping and for keeping it quiet.

Also lucky for me, Eli, who has been abducted by aliens twenty-eight times over the past two years, is better than anyone else at using the Dewey decimal numbers to find exactly what he needs in the library. The Dewey numbers, as everyone knows, are an alien plan to organize our books for transport into outer space.

And you need someone who can read alien to use it.

So I let him find what I was looking for.

"Look here," he said, bent like a curly fry over a book. "This is what a baby looks like inside your belly when it's two months old."

The gang looked at the picture.

Then they looked at me.

"That doesn't look like Alvin," said Sam.

"It's too small," Scooter agreed. "Alvin's baby is nearly as big as the baby I have at home!"

"'Having. a. baby. changes. everything,'" Eli

read like a robot. He had been reading like this since his last abduction. It was super-duper! "'Your. body. changes.'"

The gang looked at me.

I looked at my belly.

"'Your. emotions. change,'" Eli continued. "'You. could. be. happy. one. minute. and. sad. the. next. You. might. cry. more. easily. than. usual. Your. sense. of. smell. will. also. change.'"

Then Eli flipped through the pages until he came to "Your Baby at Eight Months."

Eyes popped.

Snot ran.

Jaws fell.

The baby looked . . . well, it looked like a plucked chicken in a paint can.

And the outline of the belly was . . . well, it looked a lot like mine.

"That's you," said Pinky.

"That's your baby," said Jules.

"Alvin Two," said Nhia, breathless.

Then the gang got very, very quiet.

No one said anything.

No one knew what to say.

What do you say when the belly of someone you know is in the pages of a book?

Nothing.

You should be polite.

You should notice other things.

You should talk about something else.

"Hey, that looks like Pinky's baby," said Nhia, turning the pages back to the baby at five months.

"My baby?" asked Pinky. "I don't have a baby!"

But if you looked at the drawing of the baby at five months and then you looked at Pinky's belly, anyone could see that they were exactly the same.

"And that's Hobson's baby there!" cried Jules, pointing at the baby at seven months.

"Whaaaat?" Hobson shrieked. "I don't have a baby. I'm just chubby."

"Indoor voices, please," said the librarian.

"Right, guys?" Hobson whispered. "My mom says it's just baby fat."

Heads turned.

Shirts lifted.

"Baby fat?" cried Eli. "My mom says I have that too."

"Oh no!" said Sam. "Me too!"

"BABY FAT???" Pinky screeched. "IS THAT WHAT I THINK IT IS???"

Books dropped.

Carts spun.

Decimals shifted.

"BOYS!" said the librarian.

"Waaaaaaaaaaaaah!" cried the gang.

"I don't want to have a baby!" Pinky howled.

"I don't want my belly to burst!" Nhia sobbed.

"I don't want to look like Alvin!" Hobson cried.

What's wrong with looking like me?

"*Waaaaaaaaaaaaaah!*" The gang hollered again. "*Waaaaaaaaah!*"

There was so much commotion in the library, we all would have been busted if it hadn't been for the recess bell.

.●.●.

Once you get over the shock of being pregnant, which can take all of library hour and math class too, you have to make adjustments.

"'Eating. right. is. the. first. step. to. giving. your. baby. a. healthy. start,'" Eli read from his book at lunch. "'Do. not. skip. meals. Eating. frequently. is. the. best. way. to. have. a. well. nourished. baby.'"

"I can eat a cow," said Pinky.

"I can eat a car," said Nhia.

"I can eat a school bus," said Hobson, who eats everything.

"Alvin can beat all of you," said Sam. "He can eat a house."

Eyes swiveled to my belly.

Did I look *that* big?

"'Follow. your. cravings,'" Eli continued.

"'If. you. want. to. eat. something. eat. it. Your. body. knows. what. it. needs. Listen. to. your. body.'"

"I could eat an ice cream cone," said Sam.

"I could eat three," said Scooter.

"I could eat five," said Hobson, who looks like he could eat more than that.

"Oh yeah?"

"Yeah!"

So we got ice cream cones and heaped them in front of us.

"I could eat twelve and a half," said Pinky. "In one minute flat."

"Eeeeeeeuw!" said the girls at the next table. "That's gross."

That's nothing.

I could beat them all. NO problem.

So it was a good thing I had my life savings with me or I never could have competed in the WICCC (World Ice Cream Cone Challenge) and found out who could eat more ice cream cones than anyone else.

And who could make the girls scream loudest.

CHAPTER FIVE

Personal Donations Kit

the problem with eating six cones and a lick in one minute flat, even when you're eating for two, is that you don't feel so well afterwards. In fact, you feel quite hairy. And there's something about growing hair on the backs of your hands that makes you want to scratch and howl.

Arrrrrrrruuuuuuuuuuu!

If I had been at home, it would have been a sad, wolfy cry at the moon. But I was at school, where I can't make a sound no matter how hard I try. My mouth opened. My neck stuck out. But it was a silent, airless howl.

"Alvin?" said Miss P. "Are you okay?"

Miss P's very nice. But she has a habit of calling on you when it's a full moon.

I made no eye contact.

I kept my belly in plain sight.

"Fauntleroy?" said Miss P, using Pinky's real name. "Are you okay?"

Buuuuurp! Pinky was pretty hairy too. He had had six cones in one minute flat, losing the world title to me by a lick.

And the rest of the gang . . . well, you could see the whites of their eyes, which in a normal town would be okay, but this is Concord, birthplace of the American Revolutionary War.

"Can anyone tell me which American Revolutionary War

battle made famous the order 'Don't fire until you see the whites of their eyes'?" Miss P asked.

Silence.

"We talked about this yesterday," Miss P said.

Silence.

"Does the Battle of Bunker Hill sound familiar?"

It was history class, which in a normal town, where nothing happened, might be very quiet, but in Concord, where everything happened and everyone buried explosives in their gardens and rolled howitzers about like baby carriages and guys firing muskets ran out of their homes at a moment's notice, history is the liveliest class of all!

But not today.

"Did the battle actually take place on Bunker Hill?" Miss P continued.

Silence.

"Why were the colonials told not to fire at the Redcoats 'until you see the whites of their eyes'?" Miss P asked.

Silence.

Miss P looked around. "What's going on?" she asked. "Why is everyone so quiet?"

"The boys had too much lunch," Flea said.

"They were eating for two, like Alvin," Esha added.

Then the girls giggled.

"Oh," said Miss P. "Well, let's switch to current events and come back to history. You'll all feel more awake after you give your current events reports."

Reports?

What reports?

Sam and Nhia waddled to the front of the room.

"Our report is on the capture of Paul Revere," Sam burped.

Miss P scratched her head with a pencil. "Is that current?" she asked. "Or is that history?"

The clock on the wall went *tick, tick, tick*.

No one breathed.

No one said a word.

No one wanted to be rude to Miss P. My

dad said that it's rude to correct a person, especially in front of others. I think it's one of the rules of being a gentleman, but I can't be sure. I don't remember.

But someone ought to tell her that history in Concord repeats itself. Lots of things happened here a long time ago, and they always happen again. Most events are on a regular schedule, like Paul Revere's dangerous bike ride and the start of the American Revolutionary War.

"What's current?" Sam finally asked.

"Something that happened recently," Miss P said. "It may have occurred last week, or last year, or even a few years ago, but people are still dealing with it today."

"The capture of Paul Revere is so current, it hasn't happened yet!" Nhia said.

Miss P looked puzzled.

"You see, Sam and I were riding our bikes along the Battle Road Trail," Nhia continued, "and we stopped at the place where Paul Revere is *going* to be captured during his midnight bike ride. And he was rehearsing for his capture, so we watched and took pictures."

"The two guys that were riding with him were younger and faster and got away," said Sam.

"They had mountain bikes," Nhia added. "But Paul was an old guy on a rickety bike. It's no wonder he gets busted!"

Miss P's glasses slipped on her nose. She looked at the photographs. Then she looked at Sam and Nhia. Then she sat down. She didn't look so well, but that's what happens when you're new to teaching, or new to Concord, my dad says. You have to get adjusted.

Then Flea hopped up from her chair next to me. "Psst. C'mon, Alvin," she said. "It's our turn."

Our turn?

Since when did I do a report with Flea? If I had known that I was assigned to do a project with a girl, I would have died of Embarrassment Syndrome and stayed home from school!

"Our report is on the earthquake in Haiti," Flea said in her loud voice, which goes in your ears and sits there like a sofa.

"The earthquake was scary, but the devastation was SCARIER," said Flea, making a large sweeping motion with her arms. I ducked.

"It happened a few years ago, but it still looks like the disaster struck yesterday," she said. She clicked the control button and a bright light shot out of the projector.

Everyone gasped.

I was the whiteboard. Earthquake rubble spread across my belly.

"Nearly all of the schools collapsed," Flea continued. "Fortunately, most of the children had already gone home."

I stood very still.

"People lost their homes," Flea said. "Many died. Many were badly injured."

Flea stopped. She blinked. She caught her breath.

But her breath caught her too, like a net sweeping up a butterfly. Her mouth opened, but her next words floated silently away.

A tear slipped from Flea's one good eye and rolled down her cheek.

"Thousands of children became orphans," she whispered. Another tear leaked out of Flea's eye. Her chin wrinkled. Then she began to really cry.

Oh no.

I had nothing to do with it. But it sure looked like I did. I was standing next to her and I was a boy. And boys, as everyone knows, are guilty, just like that.

Miss P gave her a tissue and a hug. "You're very brave to tell us about the tragedy," she said to Flea.

Then Miss P asked, "Do you have anything to add, Alvin?"

Miss P's very nice. She knows

I can't talk in school, but she always gives me a chance. If she ignored me once in a while it would be okay, especially when I'm TFOIC (Too Full of Ice Cream) and standing next to a weepy girl.

Flea wiped her eye. "My mom said we can help the children by sending them money to buy books and rebuild their schools."

"What a thoughtful idea," said Miss P. "Our school could take up a collection . . . in fact, we can start it right here in our class."

Flea nodded. Her one good eye began to move again. It was not a good sign. I needed an escape plan—fast! I bent down past my belly to get it from my PDK.

Then Flea's eye stopped.

I didn't actually see her eye stop, but I could *feel* it. Her glare was fixed like a blade of sun through a magnifying glass.

"Maybe we can use Alvin's PDK to hold our

donations," said Flea, sounding like her cheerful self again. "It could be our Personal Donations Kit—our PDK!"

Our WHAAAT?

I looked down. There in my PDK was my entire life savings (minus the ice cream money that was in my pockets), sparkling and twinkling at me, with some green bills among the shiny coins—like pirates' loot!

Miss P gasped. "Why, Alvin," she cried. "Is that why you brought all your money to school? You've already started the collection!"

Flea beamed.

"I'm so proud of you!" said Miss P. She clasped her hands over her heart. Then she reached for her purse. "Please allow me to be the first from our class to add to your funds."

Then she dropped a TWENTY-DOLLAR bill into my PDK.

Flea said, "I have something I can give!" She

pulled a dollar from her pocket and threw it into my PDK.

Before I knew it, everyone was throwing in what they had—quarters, dimes, nickels and pennies rained into my PDK.

Normally, I'd be jumping for joy to get so much money!

But this was not normal.

My money was mixed up with everyone else's. I couldn't tell what belonged to me and what was a donation to help the earthquake victims. My PDK, which was supposed to help me survive disasters, *was* a disaster!

Worse, my PDK looked *happy* as a Personal Donations Kit. It was kicking butt!

What do you do when that happens?

Nothing.

A gentleman never takes back his gift. It's one of the rules, I think.

And Miss P was right.

I was no longer in a food coma from lunch.

But I wished I were.

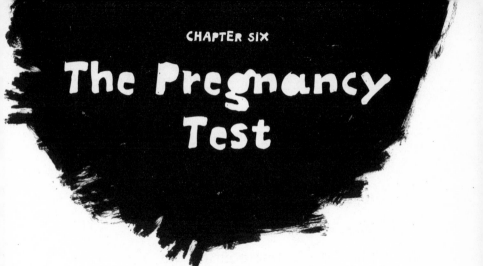

CHAPTER SIX

The Pregnancy Test

i cried all the way home.

I cried all the way up our driveway.

I cried all the way into our kitchen for my afternoon snack with GungGung and Anibelly. But Calvin went straight to our room and skipped the snack, saying he'd had enough of my wailing.

I even cried extra for Lucy to kiss me.

I cried so long and so hard that I kind of nearly forgot why I was crying, until Anibelly reminded me.

"Where's your PDK?" she asked.

"PDK?

"What PDK?

"*Waaaaaaaaaaaaaaaaaaaaaaaaah!*"

Then it all came pouring out—how I was a clever boy to take all my money to school, how I didn't spend it all on ice cream, how I didn't gamble it away in the boys' room.

"Hmmm," said GungGung, nodding and looking at me over his bowl of stinky tofu. "Mmmm...errrr... aaah...mmmm."

That's the problem with stinky tofu. It's so yummy, it's hard to get your words out.

Fortunately, it's not hard to understand my gunggung. He and I can practically read each other's minds! And it sure sounded like he was going to take me straight back to school and explain everything to Miss P and have her return my PDK, or else!

My gunggung's the best. I can tell him anything and he always understands.

"Fhanks, GrrrGrrr!" I said, after stuffing the last bite into my mouth. Then I wrapped my arms around my gunggung like a pair of chopsticks around a piece of tofu.

"A donation is a wonderful gift," said Gung-Gung. "I'm really proud of you."

Then GungGung wiped his damp forehead and headed to the sofa in the living room.

"I hope you'll consider making more donations in the future," he said, lying down and closing his eyes.

I didn't know what to say.

GungGung had given me most of that money. He always gives us *hung baus* on holidays and birthdays. So I was shocked to hear that he didn't want to help me get it back.

ZZZZZzzzzzzzzzzz. My gunggung snored.
ZZZZzzzzzzz.

The trouble with my gunggung is that he can fall asleep just like that, especially after his afternoon snack.

But not me. I ran back into the kitchen, where I grabbed a couple of sticky donuts—one for my mouth and another for my hand. Then I hurried upstairs. Anibelly and Lucy followed close behind.

"Caalviiin!" I cried, bursting into my room.

Silence.

"Calvin?"

I bit the donut.

Then POW!

I bit the carpet.

Something had knocked me smack in the back of my head.

And I was down for the count.

"Oops," I heard Calvin say. "It

wasn't supposed to work that way. He was supposed to turn around and take it on the chin."

"Is he dead?" Anibelly asked. Her soft breaths tickled the back of my neck.

"He looks much more than dead," said Calvin. "But I was aiming to stun, not kill."

Calvin and Anibelly rolled me over.

Lucy kissed the crumbs off my face.

I cracked open an eye.

Calvin was holding the spring-loaded boxing glove we'd gotten from Uncle Dennis last Christmas.

I rubbed the back of my head.

"Ouch," I said. "That wasn't very nice."

"I was testing my trap for the burglar," said Calvin.

"What trap?" I asked.

"That trap," said Calvin, pointing to a

contraption he'd rigged over the door to our room. It included both our plastic samurai swords, a broom, a hamster wheel (from our hamster who died), a hamster water bottle, spoons, marbles, balls, books, baseball cards, an umbrella, a flyswatter, sneakers, an old bike tire, strings, rope, underwear, an alarm clock, our old karaoke machine, my Tahitian drum and a couple of Lucy's chew bones. It was fantastic!

"It's a Rube Goldberg device," Calvin said.
"We're learning about them in school."

"What's Ruby's Gold Bird advice?" Anibelly asked.

"It's the most extraordinary invention your imagination can think of—to do a simple task in the most complicated way possible," Calvin said. "You have to be a genius to come up with one."

If anyone's a genius in our house, it's Calvin, that's for sure. He knows something about practically everything, and if he hasn't read about it online, he'll invent it on the spot, just like that.

"The only problem," Calvin continued, "is attaching the boxing glove in a way that doesn't kill him."

"Why don't you want to kill him if he's broken into our house?" I asked.

"Because a dead body is hard to move," said Calvin. "If I can't move it, I'll end up in prison!"

"Oh," I said. It's a good thing Calvin thought of that. I wouldn't mind so much if he had to go to prison on account of I would get to play with his stuff while he's gone, but having a dead body in my room would freak me out!

"Cal?" I said.

"Mmm," said Calvin.

"Can guys have babies?"

Calvin stopped. "What does that have to do with catching the thief?" he asked.

"Can they?" I asked.

"Of course," said Calvin. "I know kids who have two daddies."

"Oh." It was not good news.

"Alvin has a baby in his tummy," Anibelly blurted. "Just like Mom."

Calvin's mouth fell open.

"Mom says I'm simply pathetic pregnant," I said glumly.

"I've heard of that," said Calvin. He ran to the computer.

"What's going to happen to me?" I sobbed. "How long is this going to last?"

I took another bite of donut.

Calvin clicked and scrolled.

"Listen to this," said Calvin. "Did you know that the lowest penalty for driving above the speed limit in Massachusetts is a hundred-dollar fine?"

I shook my head no.

"I'm never going to drive above the speed limit, that's for sure," said Calvin. "Except in an emergency."

When Calvin's not reading the encyclopedia online, he's reading and rereading the Massachusetts drivers' manual, which is bookmarked so he can get to it with just one click. He's not old enough to drive without getting busted, but he said there's no law against knowing the rules, just in case.

Calvin clicked again.

"Did you know that the speed of blood is 2,540 miles per hour?" Calvin asked.

"WHAT DOES THAT HAVE TO DO WITH BEING PREGNANT?" I cried.

That's the problem with Calvin. He likes to look at everything.

"A hamster gestates for sixteen days," Calvin read. "A rabbit for thirty-one."

"Oooh, I like hamsters and rabbits," said Anibelly. "They're cute."

"What's gestate?" I asked.

"It means to carry something important inside of you," Calvin said. "Like a baby or an idea."

Then Calvin whistled. "An elephant gestates for twenty-two months," he said. "That's nearly almost TWO years!"

"I'M NOT AN ELE-PHANT!!!" I cried.

Then I really cried.

"*Oooooowooooo!*" Lucy howled with me.

"Okay, okay," said Calvin. "A dog gestates for sixty days. And a normal human pregnancy lasts nine months."

"Nine months???!!!"

"But a sympathetic pregnancy can last an indefinite, unspecified amount of time," Calvin added.

"What does that mean?" I asked.

"Not exactly sure," said Calvin. "Symptoms come and go, and can be more acute than an actual pregnancy."

"I love cute," said Anibelly.

"I hate cute," I said.

"Are you constipated?" Calvin asked.

"What?"

"You know, can you poop?" Calvin asked again.

"That's gross and personal," I said.

"It's the pregnancy test," Calvin said. "Answer yes to one or more of these questions and you pass. I heard Mom say that taking the test is the only way to know for sure whether you're pregnant."

Oh.

"Do you have to pee all the time?" Calvin continued.

"Yup, he sure does," Anibelly answered before I could. She smiled. "He always makes it in time too!"

Oh brother.

"Do you have gas?"

Silence.

"Not the kind you put in your car," Calvin said.

"Sometimes," I said.

"Have you gained weight?" Calvin asked. But he knew that I knew that he knew that he didn't have to ask.

"Do you have constant fatigue? Dizziness, moodiness or foot growth?"

"My feet will grow?" I asked.

"The belly isn't the only part of you that will expand," Calvin read. "Your feet will grow too."

I looked at my feet. They looked the same as they had that morning.

"Will they get hairy too?" I asked. "Like Hobbits'?"

"It doesn't say anything about that," said Calvin.

"Too bad," I said.

"Yeah," said Calvin. "I wouldn't mind having feet like that."

"It'd be nicer if you got a merboy's tail instead," said Anibelly. "Then we can play mermaids."

"Grrrrrr," I growled. I hate mermaids. And Anibelly is always trying to get me to play mermaids with her.

Then Calvin looked me smack in the eye. "You pass," he said. "Everything that happens to Mom will happen to you."

But Calvin didn't have to say. In the pit of my muffin top, I already knew.

Then, out of the corner of my eye, I saw my mom's Grocery Getter screeching up our driveway. She was home early! I love it when she comes home early. It was the best thing to happen all day.

I popped the last piece of donut into my mouth and ran downstairs.

CHAPTER SEVEN

A Scary Surprise

my mom was panting in the kitchen.

It was not a good sign.

I'd seen it on TV. When the panting starts, the baby is fast on its way! Then a commercial comes on.

"Is the baby coming now?" I asked, picking a mochi cake off the table and popping it into my mouth.

"I hope not," said my mom, putting a hand on her tummy, which made me put my hand on mine.

"I didn't come home early for the baby," she said breathlessly. "I came home early for you."

"Me?" I swallowed.

"I have a surprise planned for you," my mom said.

A surprise? Mochi cake crumbs shot out of my nose.

"Hooray!" said Anibelly. "A surprise!"

I hate surprises. They freak me out. But Anibelly loves them.

"What is it?" I asked.

"I know! I know!" Anibelly shrieked. "But I'm not going to tell."

"I think it would be really nice if you had something that was all your own before the baby came," my mom said. "Something that would be fun, with lots of physical activity."

"Physical activity?" I asked. "In my condition?"

"Well, that's exactly why," my mom said. "You'll feel more like your old self again when you're in better shape."

Huh?

"Your brother has karate and baseball and all his after-school clubs," my mom continued. "And Anibelly has circus arts and thriller lessons. But you've just been hanging with me, running errands, and not complaining."

"But that's what I like to do," I said.

It's true. Running errands with my mom is not just running errands. She always tells me something about herself that I didn't know before, such as, "Did you know that I've walked across the Mississippi River on foot?" while pushing a cart at the grocery store. Or "Did you know that I've stood within inches of the right arm of John the Baptist?" while picking up Anibelly at day care. Or "Did you know that I held an original manuscript of Thoreau's at the library yesterday?" while throwing laundry into the wash.

My mom put her arm around me.

"I know, darling," she said. "I like it too. And I appreciate that you've been helping me and watching out for me even though you didn't know I was pregnant. You have good instincts. You're a great helper and protector."

I nodded. I love it when my mom has a good word for me.

"But you're a growing boy," she said. "You need to run around and let off steam."

"A surprise, a surprise!" Anibelly sang. "Alvin's going to play hockey! Alvin's going to play hockey!"

HOCKEY?

HOCKEY???!!!

Why didn't she just sign me up for sudden death? And bury me immediately afterward?

"It's a great winter sport," my mom said. "Many kids your age are getting involved. You'll love it once you give it a try."

"But—" I started to say.

But it was too late.

"I got such a bargain on your equipment," my mom said, dragging a large bag from behind the door. "One of the moms at yoga said her son Dominic outgrew his gear and that it was the perfect size for you. She said if you want to play, you can have it."

Dominic? His real name is No Teeth. He's in the third grade.

He lost a few teeth playing hockey.

So his smile looks like a checkerboard.

And he finks he's funny when he can't say Fanksgiving or somefing.

I used to think he was funny too.

Super-duper funny.

Until . . . my mom pulled out his equipment from the bag and started putting it on me. . . .

On went his long under-wear.

On went his socks.

On went his cup.

On went his shin guards.

On went his garter belt.

On went his hockey pants.

On went his outer hockey socks.

On went his skates.

"When you learn to dress yourself," my mom said, "remember to put your skates on before putting on the top part or you'll have a hard time bending over."

Then on went the top part:

    Shoulder pads.

    Elbow pads.

    Jersey.

    Neck guard.

    Mouth guard.

    Helmet.

    Gloves.

    Stick.

"Wow," said Anibelly. "You look like a marshmallow!"

"He's a Mite," my mom said. "The youngest hockey players are called Mites."

I was a mite in a marshmallow, puffy and quiet.

How they ever shoved me into the car, I have no idea.

"Did you know that I used to play on the women's hockey team in college?" my mom said as we drove away.

I said nothing.

How can you say anything when your teeth are stuck together in one place where they can all be knocked out in a single crack?

•◦•◦•

If you want to play hockey, you have to know how to skate.

First I skated forwards. Then I skated backwards. (I've had lots of practice on Walden Pond.) The coach was very pleased. Then he asked me to skate with a stick.

Skating with a stick is tricky. It's longer than your legs.

It's *way* longer than your arms.

It feels like you're pushing around a very long, dangerous weapon.

And it gets in the way, a LOT.

You could impale yourself on it (marshmallow on a stick).

You could impale someone else on it (two marshmallows on a stick).

How you're supposed to pretend it's only a broom for sweeping a puck, I have no idea. There aren't even bristles to hide the fact that it's a skewer for roasting marshmallows, which made me feel hungry again.

"Every time you go out there, I want you to do one thing better," the coach said.

The team nodded.

"We play as a team," the coach

said. "We practice as a team. Help each other out. Help the new kid out."

That's me. I'm the new kid.

If there's anything I like about hockey, it's this: It's a silent game. No one talks, or screams or yells. All the players' teeth are stuck together.

If there's anything else I like about hockey, it's this: The spectators are not silent at all. They're very loud!

"Skate, Alvin, skate!" my mom yelled.

"C'mon, Alvin!" Anibelly screamed. "Skate fast!"

It was super-duper!

But if there's anything I don't like about hockey, it's this: There's a girl on my team.

"Hi, Alvin!" she said with her one good eye.

It was Flea.

But her helmet said "FEAR-LESS," which is EARLESS with an "F" in front.

Yikes!

Why hadn't I ever noticed that about her before?

I wondered where she had lost her ears!

"Do this!" she said with her eye. She controlled a puck down the rink like it was attached to her stick.

Then she crashed into the boards and fell, *hard*.

But she's not delicate. She's a pirate. She got right up and practiced again.

But the worst thing about hockey is this: Hockey, as everyone knows, is death by multiple choice. You can die by:

a. puck
b. blade
c. stick
d. Zamboni
e. all of the above

But not me. I died by:

f. humiliation

"He'd make the perfect goalie," the coach

told my mom. "He's got good instincts . . . and his size covers most of the goal mouth."

My SIZE?

It was the worst ending to the worst day of my life.

CHAPTER EIGHT

The Trouble with Naming a Baby

embarrassing news travels fast.

By the time it was recess the next morning, I was the goalkeeper for a soccer game on the playground.

"Alvin's a wall!" cried Nhia.

"Nothing gets past him!" said Scooter.

"Amazing," said Pinky. "He just stands there!"

How the gang found out, I have no idea.

I wanted to cry!

But you can't cry and eat at the same time. And I'd rather eat. So I popped one of my pohpoh's mochi cakes into my mouth. I had an emergency supply of them in my pocket, just in case.

"Hey, guys, listen to this," said Eli, who was the only one not playing. He was reading his book.

"'Naming. your. newborn. baby. is. one. of. the. most. important. decisions. you. will. make. for. your. child.'"

Wham! The ball came flying and hit him on the head. The gang rushed over.

"Ow!" Eli said, without looking up. He didn't even rub the spot. He kept his finger on the page, and he kept reading. "'A. name. affects. the. way. we. think. of. ourselves. and. the. way. others. see. us.'"

"I'm naming my baby Mario," said Sam.

"Mine is going to be Sonic," said Nhia.

I like Tiger, I wanted to say, but nothing came out of my mouth.

"I like Tiger," said Pinky.

"Name him something else," said Hobson, who always gives you a choice. "Or don't name him at all."

"Tiger's mine," said Pinky.

"MINE!" Hobson said.

Before he could see it coming, Hobson fell on top of Pinky, like a house sailing out of the clear blue sky and landing right on top of the wicked witch. It was super-duper!

Too bad the end-of-recess bell rang just then and we had to hurry in.

.●.●.

Miss P had some good news for us after lunch.

"Guess how much we collected in donations for earthquake relief yesterday?" Miss P asked.

I had no idea.

I made no eye contact.

But I eyed my PDK that was sitting on top of her desk.

"One hundred twenty-two dollars and eighty-four cents!" said Miss P, clapping her hands.

Everyone clapped.

"Almost all of that was Alvin's money," Flea said proudly.

"Indeed," said Miss P. "Alvin's an inspiration to us all."

I sat a little taller.

"When the other classes heard about our collection," Miss P continued, "they made their own Personal Donations Kits, and have already collected nearly three hundred dollars.

"You should be very proud of yourselves,"

Miss P said. "You started something that could help a lot of kids."

Everyone sat taller.

"In fact, your principal thought it was such a good idea that she wants to get other schools involved," Miss P added. "She called the local TV station, and emailed your parents for permission for a news crew to do a story on us this afternoon."

Everyone squealed with excitement.

Everyone, that is, except me.

Who wants to be on TV?

Not me!!!

My dad says when you have *that* much money sitting around, drawing attention to it is a ticket to trouble with a capital "T."

•◉•◉•

This is how to know you are on the express train to Trouble.

You can't hear your lessons.

You ask for the bathroom pass.

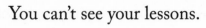

You can't see your lessons.

You ask for the bathroom pass.

You can't taste your emergency mochi cakes.

You ask for the bathroom pass.

"Alvin," said Miss P. "Don't you think that's enough of going to the bathroom for now?"

Miss P's very nice. She smells like fresh laundry and lets you use the bathroom pass as often as you need, just in case.

But the look on her face said that using the pass every three seconds was pushing your luck, mister.

So I sat down.

I didn't ask for the bathroom pass.

But now I was *sure* I needed to go, not like the other times when I only *thought* I needed to go.

Gulp.

Worse, I had no idea why the girl next to me was smiling at me. It was the same girl who was FEARLESS. Only now she had ears. And you know when a girl who can regrow her ears just like that smiles at you, it's Trouble.

"Alvin," she said.

Was she talking to me?

"I made you something," said Flea.

She held out a basket. It looked like it could be a picnic basket (good). Or it could be a basket for *girl* things (bad). It was hard to tell.

"It's your new PDK," she said.

I could hardly believe it! I've had to use my pockets ever since my PDK became the Personal Donations Kit.

"Your Pregnancy Disaster Kit!" Flea whispered.

Heads turned.

I had no idea what lesson we were doing, but Flea, as usual, was already done with her assignment. She opened the basket and pulled out:

A blankie.

Hand sanitizer.

Diaper cream.

An old stuffed tiger.

Cheese 'n' crackers.

A diaper.

A Mozart CD.

An emergency plan:

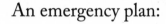

How to Take Care of Your Baby

① Wrap it in the blanket.
② Use hand sanitizer.
③ Use cream on the butt.
④ Put the butt on the diaper.
⑤ Eat cheese 'n' crackers (but see #2 first).
⑥ Play Mozart CD.
⑦ Don't panic.
⑧ Be a good daddy!

I ignored her.

I ignored the basket, which was not a PDK, but a BDK—a Baby Diapering Kit! I wanted to tell her this, but my mouth felt like it was filled with diaper cream.

I ignored Pinky, who was snickering.

I ignored everything except the screaming voice inside that was telling me how frightful being on TV was going to be.

I was so good at ignoring things that I almost missed the first snowflake at 12:57, just as Miss P was handing out another worksheet.

Then I saw another flake at 1:01.

Then two flakes at 1:06, one right after the other. It was super-duper!

It was practically a nor'easter! And it was about to save us from being on TV!

The brakes on the fast train to Trouble squeal to a stop.

I look out the train window.

An avalanche pours from the

sky, like oatmeal flakes from the overhead food bin at the grocery store.

The school is buried by the storm of the millennium!

Bulldozers arrive.

Parents cry.

Policemen panic.

Mammoths roam the earth.

"Alvin," a voice said. "Are you still with us?"

Miss P has a habit of calling on you just when the New Ice Age arrives.

I snapped out of it in time to see three flakes fall at 1:08.

This time *everyone* saw them.

And rushed to the windows.

Outside, a TV crew was interviewing our principal in front of the school.

She was probably announcing an early dismissal!

Hooray! I felt like dancing!

But Miss P said a few flakes was nothing to get excited about and that we should sit down and be on our best behavior because the TV people were about to interview us.

Gulp.

And before I knew it, a video camera came into our room. Then a lady with a microphone. Then a very bright light, like the kind you should avoid on account of it can only mean one thing: You're dead.

"We're here today with a special class and a very special young man," the lady began.

I squinted into the light.

"A second grader gave up his life savings and inspired his entire school to make donations to help earthquake victims in Haiti," said the lady.

Flea sprang from her seat next to me. "That's right, that's him right there," she said, pointing at me.

The lady smiled.

"I did the report," Flea said. "But it was Alvin

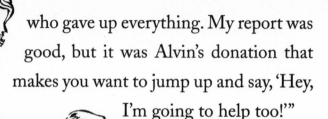

who gave up everything. My report was good, but it was Alvin's donation that makes you want to jump up and say, 'Hey, I'm going to help too!'"

"How does it feel to be an in-spiration?" the lady asked.

"It feels great!" Flea an-swered for me. "Alvin's a perspiration to everyone." Her one good eye sparkled like a marble.

"I mean, Alvin never says anything in school or does anything well," Flea continued. "He doesn't pay attention. He can't punch-you-wait. He never remembers his library book. My mom says never underestimate a kid like that—they could amaze you."

The big glass eye of the camera looked smack into the bottom of me.

My liver twisted.

My vision blurred.

"Who would ever have guessed that Alvin would give away all his money to help people so far away?" Flea asked. "He even gave away his PDK!" Her arm flew up in a big exclamation mark. "But I made sure he got another one," she added.

"Another one?" asked the lady.

"I made him a Pregnancy Disaster Kit!" Flea said, pointing to the thing under my desk.

"A what?" said the lady.

"He's pregnant, you know," Flea said, smiling proudly. "That's why he's so big."

The classroom spun one way.

My desk spun in the other.

The only thing that kept me from DDOTS (Dropping Dead on the Spot), was—I saw it out of the corner of my eye—another snowflake.

CHAPTER NINE

Gone, Just Like That

maybe being on tv wasn't so bad after all.

That night, my mom watched the five o'clock news.

"Oh, Alvin!" she cried. "This is beautiful."

Then she really cried.

My mom's that way. She cries at movies. She cries at books. And she cries when something is so beautiful that it makes you want to hug the world.

She pressed a button and watched the news again.

There I was; my face filled the screen.

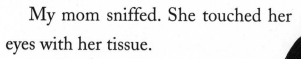

"Hey, there's Alvin!" Anibelly said, for the fiftieth time. She was so excited.

My mom sniffed. She touched her eyes with her tissue.

"Oh, Alvin," my mom said again. "I just love this. I can't believe you did something so magnanimous."

I couldn't believe I did something so magnetic either.

That was the good news.

The bad news was that the next day was not a snow day.

But it was not a normal, ordinary day either.

"Did someone hide our PDK?" Miss P asked first thing in the morning. "Where's our PDK?"

She looked under her desk.

We looked in our art supply cabinet.

We pulled out our science supply drawers.

Then Miss P picked up the phone and called the principal.

Worse, the principal said all the other PDKs were missing too.

Gone.

Overnight.

Just like that.

It was the worst thing that had ever happened at our school.

Then the police arrived with the K9 unit.

It was the best thing that had ever happened at our school.

The dog sniffed everywhere. It was super-duper!

Then the fingerprint dusting kit came out.

Black powder clouds filled the air. It was fantastic!

But the news from our principal later in the day was not so good.

"The police said that whoever stole our donations for earthquake relief is the same person who has been breaking into homes," Miss Madhaven said. "Fingerprints here matched fingerprints from homes that were burglarized."

Everyone gasped.

Then fell silent.

Except for Flea. She jumped from her seat and blurted, "If we hadn't gotten on TV yesterday, we'd still have our PDK! The thief got the idea from watching the news!"

I could have told her that.

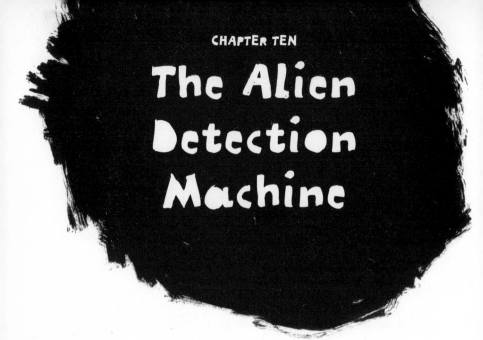

CHAPTER TEN

The Alien Detection Machine

"mommmmmmmmm!!!" I screamed all the way up my driveway as soon as I got off the bus.

I can never remember which days my mom works from home and which days she works in an office. I just know that some afternoons my gunggung is there to watch us, and other afternoons my mom is home. It's always a surprise. Today, her Grocery Getter was in the garage, which is a dead giveaway.

"MOMMMMMMMMMM!!!" I chased my

voice into the house. I was going so fast, Ani-belly jumped out of my way—right before I crashed like a flying squirrel without brakes into my mom's arms.

"Alvin," I heard my mom say before I burst into tears.

"WAAAAAAAAAAAAAAAAAAAAAAH!!!" I cried. "WAAAAAAAAAAAAAAAAAAAAAA-AAAAAAAAAAAAH!!!"

I clung to my mom and sobbed.

"It's.

"All.

"Gone."

Then I sank into my mom and cried some more.

"I know, darling," said my mom, holding me tight. "Miss Madhaven called and told me. I'm very sorry."

"It's not faaaaaaaaair," I bellowed.

"Ooooowoooooo!" Lucy cried.

"It was a LOT of money," I said. "And MOST of it was MINE!"

My mom nodded.

She smoothed my hair.

She rubbed my back.

"I'm sorry," my mom said. "When bad things happen, it's always unfair."

"*Waaaaaaaaaaah!*" I cried. "*Waaaaaaaaaaah!*"

My mom held me close.

I didn't want her to let go, ever.

I stayed in her lap and leaned against her big, round belly and didn't say anything. And Anibelly hugged me from the other side and

didn't say anything either. I love it when she does that.

But maybe the baby did not.

First it was round.

Then it was square.

Then it poked me in the eye.

"Older moms like you face a greater chance of having something wrong with the baby, don't they?" I blurted. "That's what the kids at school said. It was in a book."

Anibelly gasped.

I'm not sure Anibelly should have heard it, but she did. Her ears were open, like two car doors, one on each side. And the scary news hopped in and buckled itself right in.

"Please don't worry," my mom said, giving both of us a hug. "Our baby is healthy and fine.

"Alvin," my mom said gently. "You can't worry about every little thing."

But I was. I was very worried.

And I put some fear in Anibelly too, I'm sure of it.

And when you've done that, you know what's coming next.

Psycho therapy.

• ● • ● •

Anibelly had never needed psycho therapy before, but she sure looked like she needed it now. So I read her the rules before we left:

How to Go to Psycho Therapy
Quietly.
Get in the car.
Buckle in.
Say something nice.
Say something else nice.
No firecrackers.
No flying out the window.

"I sure wish Anibelly and I could be home playing right now," I said nicely from the backseat of the car.

My mom said nothing.

Anibelly said nothing.

"I sure wish I weren't missing my calligraphy lesson with GungGung," I said, also very nicely. Calvin was at an after-school club, and normally, GungGung, Anibelly and I would be doing some sort of ancient Chinese torture at home, like calligraphy or ribbon dancing.

My mom looked at me in the rearview mirror.

"When's the next hockey practice?" I asked, nicest of all.

Then surprise, surprise! When we arrived at the doctors' building, we didn't go through the frightful door where the psycho works as a therapist.

We went through a different door.

We sat down.

I looked around.

There I was with Anibelly and my mom, in a roomful of other moms just like mine.

"Mrs. Ho," said a lady with a clipboard and a big smile.

My mom got up. "C'mon," she said, touching my arm. "It's our turn."

Our turn?

My legs were stuck like fence posts. My feet wouldn't lift. My arms wouldn't swing. My head wouldn't turn.

And poor Anibelly, she was stuck too!

My mom had to chip us off the floor and cart us in. The problem was, there was no cart. But boy, is she strong. I bet my mom could lift a couple of pianos if she wanted to!

"What a nice young gentleman you are to bring your mom," the lady with the clipboard said to me.

She weighed my mom. Then she slipped a band around my mom's arm and it squeezed my mom like a python squeezing its dinner.

"Would you like to be weighed and have your blood pressure taken too?" she asked, giving me a wink.

No way!

But wait a minute.

Maybe I'd better get checked too, just in case.

I stepped on the scale.

Clonk! went the weight.

I heard my mom gasp.

Oops.

As if that weren't scary enough, the doctor swooshed in.

"Hi, Anibelly," she said to Anibelly. "And you must be Calvin," she said to me.

I said nothing.

I made no eye contact.

"It's Alvin," said my mom.

"I don't believe it!" the doctor said. "It seems like only yesterday I delivered you!"

Delivered me? I was Chinese takeout?

"They're terribly worried about me and the baby," my mom said. "So I thought bringing them to my appointment might help."

"It always helps," said the doctor.

Rrrrrrrrrrh? said my belly.

"Oh dear," said the doctor. "You're sympathetically pregnant too!"

"He is," said my mom. Then she and the doctor looked at one another in that way that said a million things in a language I couldn't hear.

Rrrrrrrrrrh! My stomach complained even louder.

The doctor smiled. "After we take a look at your mom," she said, "we'll have a peek at you."

Then the doctor squirted something slimy on my mom's belly.

"This is an ultrasound machine," said the doctor, rolling something on my mom's skin. "It uses sound waves to look at your brother or sister growing inside your mom."

"It doesn't hurt," my mom assured us.

"Do you see the baby?" asked the doctor, pointing to the computer screen.

I looked.

"Sweetheart, I think the baby is waving to you," my mom said.

All I saw was the UFO. The same one with the search beam that's in the pictures on our refrigerator!

"Would you like to say hello?" the doctor asked. "It can hear you."

It?

I said nothing.

I don't talk to aliens.

But Anibelly does.

"Hi," said Anibelly. "I'm Anibelly Ho. I'm your big sister and we'll play mermaids together."

"The baby looks fine," the doctor said to my mom. "Everything is healthy and right on schedule."

"See, honey," said my mom, "there's nothing to worry about."

Nothing to worry about?

I was in a scary doctor's office, looking at a baby UFO inside my mom's big body.

Worse, the doctor's alien detection wand was now pointing at me!

"Would you like a quick look?" she asked. "Then you can have your very own picture to take home."

WHUUUUMP!
BOOOOONK!
CRAAAAAASH!

CHAPTER ELEVEN

Decoding Your Baby's Cries

"you're the only person who goes to the doctor's office to get *hurt,*" Calvin said. He was working on his Rudy Goldburger machine again when I got home.

I carefully touched the bump on my head.

This wasn't the first time I'd fallen or fainted or knocked something over at the doctor's office. The good news is that they can sew me right up. The bad news is that it hurts.

Worse, a bump on the head wasn't the only thing that left the doctor's office with me.

"What's that?" Calvin asked. He was gluing train tracks to our bookcase. I could swear Calvin has eyes in the back of his head; he sees everything in the room even when he's not looking.

"Nothing," I said.

"It's something," said Calvin. "C'mon, what is it?"

"A doll," I said, trying my best to hide the thing behind me.

"What are you doing with a *doll*?" Calvin asked, pulling some books out so that they sat halfway off the shelves. I love it when Calvin is in a tinkering mood. Not only is he building something useful, but he's calm and nonviolent, which is a lot better than when he comes home from karate, which always puts him in a mood to kick my butt.

"Mom's doctor loaned it to me," I said. "She said I should carry it around for a while. It'll help me get used to having a baby and make everything less scary."

"You're so lucky," said Anibelly, who was

coloring on my bed. "I wish she had given it to me."

Before I knew it, Anibelly scooped up my doll and gave it a kiss.

"I wouldn't do that," I said.

"Why not?" asked Anibelly.

"It's covered with a million germs," I said.

"But babies need kissing," said Anibelly. "You're not a good daddy."

"I'm not its daddy!" I said.

"You are."

"Am NOTTTTTTTT!" I screamed at the top of my lungs, and stamped my foot.

The doll burst out crying.

Waaaaaaaaaaaaaaaaaah!

I froze.

But Anibelly didn't. She rubbed the doll's back and rocked it gently. The crying stopped.

Anibelly smiled.

"You're a great mommy, Anibelly," said Calvin, who always has a good word for her.

"I think it has a computer chip inside," Calvin added, inspecting the doll. "It makes different cries for hunger, pain, fear, loneliness . . . and diaper change. And you have to figure out which cry means what, or else."

"Or else what?" I asked.

"Or else it'll keep crying, like a real baby," said Calvin.

Just then a racquetball dropped from the top shelf and zigzagged along the top edge of the books, setting off a train on the tracks, which dumped a load of marbles into a net, which pulled a string, which rang a bell. It was super-duper!

"What's that for?" I asked.

"That's the alarm for me to shoot," said Calvin.

"Shoot the robber?" I asked.

"Yup," said Calvin. "No one messes with donations for earthquake victims."

"I thought you didn't want a dead body," I said.

"I don't," Calvin said. "I just want to scare him so he'll give back the money."

"Oh," I said.

"When he trips the wire," said Calvin, pointing toward our door, "the ball will drop, the train will run and the alarm will sound. Then I'll shoot him."

"What are you going to shoot him with?" I asked.

"Dunno," said Calvin. "Okay, maybe that will be the alarm for me to call 911 instead.

"Anyway, the dolls are for practice," Calvin said, remembering what we were talking about before his Roob Gober device went off. "Once you crack the code, they're easy to take care of, just like a regular baby."

"What code?" I asked.

Calvin ran to the computer and I hurried after him.

Clickclickclick. Scroll.

"Here it is," said Calvin. And there on the screen was the following menu:

How to Decode Your Baby's Cries

1. Real pain: high-pitched, short, loud screams.

2. Night terrors: sudden loud shrieking.

3. Discomfort: whiny, breathy whimpering.

4. Hunger: short wails, sounds like a siren.

5. Gas: a whimpering, pushing sound or a panicky, grunting cry.

6. Tiredness: sharp, openmouthed wail.

7. Colic: piercing, howling, intense "top-of-the-lungs" scream that lasts three hours a day for three weeks.

"It's like the list of ice cream flavors at Kimball's," said Calvin. "You just pick the cry of the day!"

Calvin hit the Print button.

Then *WHUUUUMP!*

I was down for a second time in the same afternoon. And Calvin was on top of me.

The only problem with a tinkering afternoon is that it can turn into a karate one, just like that.

And I was crying numbers one through seven, all at once.

WAAAAAAAAAAAAAAAAAAAAAAAH!!!

Crying is really great no matter what number you use. You always feel better afterwards.

Except when you have a doll with the computer chip inside that cries when you do.

WAAAAAAAAAAAAAAAAAA-AAAAAAAAAAAAAAAAH!!! the doll howled.

I had no idea which flavor it was.

Or what to do.

No matter what I did, it wouldn't stop.

So I opened the window to give it some air. Whenever my dad is mad like that, he curses like crazy in Shakespeare—"Swim with leeches, thou dull and muddy-mettled rascal!" or "Eat a crocodile, thou churlish spur-galled pumpion!" Then he

storms out for air. Air is like medicine, it always makes him feel better.

But a doll can't take medicine.

WAAAAAAAAAAAAAAAAAAA-AAH! The doll cried even louder.

So I chucked it out the window.

And that was the end of that.

CHAPTER TWELVE

"I Miss You, Dad."

surviving a week without my dad is really hard.

It's the time when nothing works.

Not the tightrope I tied between two trees for Anibelly's circus arts practice.

Not Firecracker Man's lookout for burglars.

Not any of the rules for being a gentleman that I'm supposed to follow.

Not my yoga tree pose.

Not the homework side of my brain.

Nothing.

"Sounds like you're having a really rough week, son," my dad said over the phone.

It was bedtime and my dad had called to say good night. He never misses saying good night, whether he's at home or not. It was great to hear his voice, but it wasn't so great that his voice was coming out of Calvin's cell phone instead of my dad's body. I clamped the phone between my head and my shoulder, where my dad's arm belonged, but it wasn't the same.

I couldn't feel his quillery face.

I couldn't sit in his lap.

I couldn't smell him.

A hot tear rolled down my cheek.

Then another.

And another.

And before I knew it, I was crying full blast.

My dad was very quiet.

It sounded like he wasn't there, but I knew he was. My dad's a very good listener, and when he's listening he doesn't make a sound.

"ICAN'TWAITFORTHISPREGNANCY TOBEOVER!" I cried.

I thought I heard my dad chuckle, just a little, but I wasn't sure.

"IT'S A MEDICAL EMER-GENCY!" I added, just in case he didn't know. "BUTMOM'SSTILL MAKINGMEGOTOSCHOOL ANDSHEEVENSIGNEDMEUP FORHOCKEY!"

There was phone noise.

Then parts of words floated like confetti into my ears.

"Erp.

"Ark.

"Wah."

It sounded like my dad spit all his words onto the ice and cracked them with a hockey stick.

"Dad?" I said.

SSSssssssSSSSssssssSSSSSSSssssssss.

"Is Mom going to have her baby soon?" I asked.

"Rrrrreh," said my dad. "Simp . . . preg . . . great."

"What, Dad?"

"It'll . . . you . . . better man . . . son," said my dad. "You'll . . . understand . . . wa . . . yo . . . mah . . . went thr . . . for you."

Huh?

SsssssSssssSSSSSSssssssss.

"What if Mom has her baby tonight?

"What if my belly bursts?

"What if the burglar comes to our house?

"What if I die by hockey puck?"

Silence.

"I miss you, Dad," I said.

Silence.

"I wish you were home."

Silence.

"I love you!" I said loudly.

"Call ended," the screen said silently.

That's the problem with cell phones. Sometimes you have to imagine the rest of the conversation or you'll need lots of therapy to get over it, and I already go to therapy once a month, which is frightful enough.

"C'mon," said Calvin, taking back his phone. "It's time for bed."

It was time for a story. Normally, when my dad's at home, he'll read to us a true tale of indomitable courage and dangerous expeditions. When he's not home, my mom will read to us, but my mom was exhausted and had put Anibelly to bed and gone to bed herself.

"Can we read more of *The Odd Sea*?" I asked.

"It's *The* Oddest *Sea*," Calvin said. "No."

"Why not?" I asked.

"Not in the mood," said Calvin.

Calvin's that way. If he misses someone he won't do anything that reminds him of that person. Not like me. When I miss my dad, I do everything that I normally do with him to make it seem like he's not gone.

"Well, can we say some Shakespearean insults, then?" I asked.

"Thou art a burly-boned, motley-minded hedge pig!" Calvin cried.

"Thou worm of odiferous moldy biscuit!" I shrieked.

Pillows swung.

"Thou'rt by no means valiant," Calvin howled.

"For thou dost fear the soft and tender fork of a poor worm!"

"Thou bootless fly-bitten harpy!"

"Lice eater!"

"Maggot licker!"

We jumped so high on our beds we nearly crashed and broke all our bones. It was super-duper!

Then Calvin thudded into his pillow.

And I thudded into mine.

"Feel better?" Calvin asked, breathless.

"Yup," I said, gasping.

"Me too," said Calvin.

"Are you scared of everything changing too, Cal?" I asked.

"At times like this, I wish there were a courage pill," said Calvin.

"How come you don't show it?" I asked.

"I'm bigger than you," said Calvin.

"So?"

"So the bigger you are, the more you forget how to show it," Calvin said. "By the time you're as big as Dad, you could be scared to death,

but no one would ever know it until they find your body."

"Calvin?" I said.

"Go to sleep," Calvin said, rolling over. "And turn off the light."

"But I can't sleep," I said.

Silence.

"If the baby comes tonight, no one will be ready," I said.

"Zzzzzzzzz," said Calvin. "Zzzzzzzzz."

Like all the other dudes in my family, Calvin goes from emergency alert to stage three deep sleep with no rapid eye movement and no muscle activity in three seconds flat. And there's no waking him, even with a stick of dynamite.

The house was suddenly graveyard quiet.

You could hear everything.

And nothing at all.

I reset Calvin's Robber Goldbug trap, just in case.

Then I heard footsteps in the hallway.

I gasped.

Creakcreakcreak.

I grabbed my flashlight.

Tinkletinkle.

I cracked open my door.

Phroouuuuush!

It was my mom. She was sleepwalking. She has a permanent bathroom pass and goes without turning on a light and without opening her eyes.

My poor mom.

CHAPTER THIRTEEN

Sibling School

the problem with throwing one useless thing out the window is that another one is sure to come along.

Right after school the next day—surprise, surprise—my mom and Anibelly picked us up and we headed to sibling school, whatever that is, at Emerson Hospital.

"But Mom," Calvin said. "I'm not the one with issues. Alvin is."

"It'll be good for all of you," my mom said, looking at us in her rearview mirror. She was

very cheerful. "You'll learn some new skills, make some new friends and feel more prepared to have a baby join our family."

Calvin glared at me. He wanted to go home to work on his Rudy Goldthing device again, I could tell.

"What if the robber breaks in while we're gone?" Calvin asked.

"Don't worry," said my mom. "Lucy's home."

"But Lucy's friendly," he said.

"Lucy makes a lot of noise," said my mom. "She'll let the neighbors know if something's up."

"But our neighbors are never home," Calvin said.

It's true. They're three hundred years old and they have places to go and bingo to play before they die. I should know. They've asked me to keep an eye on things for them on account of that's what I do.

"Calvin," said my mom. "You can't let your fears tell you what to do."

"Why not?" Calvin asked. "Alvin does."

"Boys," said my mom. "You're both bigger than your fears."

"We're bigger than a couple of grenades too," Calvin said. "You'd fear those, wouldn't you?"

The wind blew.

The radio played.

"Lalalalalalala," sang Anibelly. "Lalalalalala."

My mom kept one eye in the mirror looking at us and one eye straight ahead. How she does that, I have no idea.

I had a feeling my mom was planning to stay for sibling school to keep an eye on me, but she dropped us off instead and turned the car around, squealing on her tires as she went.

It was really too bad.

I wouldn't have minded if she'd stayed, especially after I saw the pain chart on the wall:

Choose the Face That Best Describes How You Feel

0	2	4	6	8	10

| NO HURT | HURTS LITTLE BIT | HURTS LITTLE MORE | HURTS EVEN MORE | HURTS WHOLE LOT | HURTS WORST |

I'd had no idea that pain would be involved.

But first, there were milk and cookies.

I ate several of each kind of cookie and drank a carton of chocolate milk. It was "0, No hurt" on the pain scale.

Then we did a craft. We made picture frames for our babies. Anibelly was really into it. She made two.

Calvin got into it too. His frame looked like a Rube Goldbee device made with tongue depressors, crayons and pom-poms.

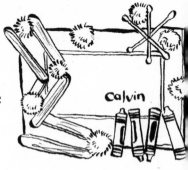

Calvin

But I'm allergic to tongue depressors. They make me gag. Even looking at one makes my mouth taste like I'd licked a toilet. So a big pile of tongue depressors was a "5, Drooling stomach acid," which was not on the chart, but it should be, so I drew my own pain chart instead of making a picture frame.

"Are you getting a baby brother or baby sister?" asked HELLO, My Name Is Jasmine.

Her question was a "3.5, Hurts like a loose tooth."

I said nothing.

I don't talk to strangers.

But Anibelly does.

"We're getting a surprise!" Anibelly said. "It's a surprise."

"I'm going to have a baby sister," said HELLO, My Name Is Jasmine. "Her name is Rose. We're

going to play mermaids together and I'm going to share my room with her and let her borrow my books and my toys and we're going to be best friends."

"That's what I want!" Anibelly said, jumping up. "I want a little sister like that!"

Then the two girls screamed and hopped up and down like a couple of spiders in a death lock. It was a "1.0, Hurts like constipation."

Next was a lesson on diapering.

It was not a play lesson, but the real lesson given to grown-ups in the new-parent class. "Diapering is sometimes a team effort," the teacher said. "You never know when you might be asked to help."

We grabbed dolls and diapers.

"Keep a hand on your baby at all times," said the teacher. "Babies squirm a lot when they're being changed."

I put a firm hand on my doll.

"Keep your baby covered," said the teacher, putting a diaper over her doll. "Especially if you have a baby boy, or you could get a surprise."

A surprise? What surprise?

Squiiiiiiiiirt!

Sibling school exploded with laughter.

Gross!!! My doll had sprayed me in the face! It was a "10, Hurts like an arrow in the head" on my pride.

Next was the tour.

"All moms get the red carpet treatment here," said the tour guide, "and yours will too."

I looked around. The floors were bare and shiny. Why were they offering a carpet treatment to moms?

While the tour guide was pointing to this and that, someone whispered, "Let's go ride the elevator!" I don't ride elevators, but if I did, I certainly wouldn't ride one that was labeled "Elevator to Clough Surgical Center," which might as well have been called "Elevator to Heaven." I had to warn them, but my voice didn't work. Fortunately I had my pain chart with me, so I pointed to "13.0, Hurts like an explosion," which shows a head in midexplosion that I had drawn with crayons. It took only a few seconds for the kids in the elevator to understand and to start screaming like chickens trapped in a lobster cage!

After that everyone looked like they were at "8.5, Hurts like a finger in a light socket." Everyone, that is, except me and Anibelly and her new friend, who never got in the elevator but were skipping down the hall hand in hand singing, "Lalalalalalalalala."

The tour guide herself was at "7.5, Hurts like a snake bite" when we reached the window where the babies were sleeping like wrapped mummies all in a row.

By the time we got to the room where the babies are born, I was at "9.0, Hurts like a smack into a tree."

"Your mom will be wheeled in here and she'll

be made as comfortable as possible on that bed," said the guide.

It didn't look comfortable to me.

In fact, the room looked like a genuine torture chamber! There were masks and gowns and

machines and devices that looked a lot more complicated than the ones Calvin made.

"What's that for?" I heard Anibelly ask. I stood on tiptoe and telescoped my neck to see what she was pointing at. It was a pair of very scary, very large salad tongs.

"It's used for babies that need a little extra help . . . ," the guide began.

"Tossed baby green salad?" Anibelly asked.

Everyone shrieked.

Then lurched.

My liver burped.

My stomach rolled.

It was hard to hear what else the tour guide was saying. I was off the chart and completely freaked out, and so was everyone else.

Lucky for me, I was standing next to a little red handle on the wall. "Emergency," it said on top. "Pull."

I don't think I need to tell you what happened next.

CHAPTER FOURTEEN

My Mom Was Getting Bigger and Bigger!

there are many ways to get out of trouble after making such a big disturbance at the hospital.

1. Cry.
2. Cry louder.
3. Let out a high-pitched, piercing, howling, intense "top-of-the-lungs" scream lasting three hours.
4. Give a gift.

I had a feeling I'd already overused numbers 1
through 3. So I made a Pregnancy Disaster Kit
for my mom. It was not like the one Flea gave
me, which was useless. This one was helpful for
going to the hospital. It contained:

A Nightgown.

Slippers.

Lipstick.

A photo of Mom and Baby Alvin.

A photo of Mom and Toddler Alvin.

A photo of Mom and Kindergarten Alvin.

A photo of Mom and Grown-Up Alvin.

(So that she wouldn't forget me.)

A water bottle.

A rope (for climbing out the window in case of fire).

A mask (to prevent smoke and germ inhalation).

A map of escape route out of the hospital (in case she changes her mind).

My pain chart.

Choose the Face That Best Describes How You Feel

> Dear Mom,
>
> By the time you read this, you'll be in the ER having your baby. This is your PDK. I packed everything you need, except shampoo. The hospital will give you a special carpet shampoo treatment! Don't be skared! But if you are, take the stares. And don't forget - I love you forever even if you're having another baby.
>
> Sincerely,
> Alvin
>
>
>
> P.S. If it's a girl, please switch for a boy!

And a letter from me.

I put it all in an overnight bag and gave it to my mom at dinner.

"Oh, Alvin," she said. "You're so thoughtful."

My mom put down her chopsticks and gave me a hug. "You're my sweet, sympathetic boy."

I am.

And it worked.

Normally, I'd be busted, but she wasn't upset with me at all!

But like I said, she wasn't normal.

My mom was getting bigger and bigger!

On a pregnancy scale, she was a "9, Ready to burst!"

After dinner, my mom was cleaning and moving furniture like crazy! We were spying on her from upstairs, where it was safe.

"I don't think Dad's going to make it home in time," Calvin said. "Pregnant ladies clean and move furniture when the baby's about to be born."

"Hooray!" said Anibelly.

"What are we going to do?" I asked.

"Plan B," said Calvin, running to our room.

"What's Plan B?" I asked, running after him.

"If Dad isn't back in time to drive her," Calvin said, "Mom could end up having her baby here."

"In our room?"

"Yup," said Calvin. "If we turn our room into a birthing room, it'll be nice and comfortable for her and the baby."

"Hooray!" Anibelly said again. "We'll make it nicer than the one at the hospital."

"Let's draw a plan for it," Calvin said.

So we did. Here's what it looked like:

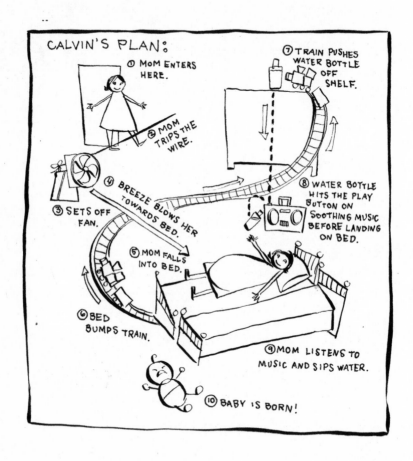

CALVIN'S PLAN:

① MOM ENTERS HERE.

② MOM TRIPS THE WIRE.

③ SETS OFF FAN.

④ BREEZE BLOWS HER TOWARDS BED.

⑤ MOM FALLS INTO BED.

⑥ BED BUMPS TRAIN.

⑦ TRAIN PUSHES WATER BOTTLE OFF SHELF.

⑧ WATER BOTTLE HITS THE PLAY BUTTON ON SOOTHING MUSIC BEFORE LANDING ON BED.

⑨ MOM LISTENS TO MUSIC AND SIPS WATER.

⑩ BABY IS BORN!

It was super-duper!

But we had no time to lose.

First, we pushed our beds together.

"*Rrrrrf, rrrrrf!*" said Lucy, who was supervising everything.

Then we took all our blankets and made a nest. Lucy added her blanket. And Anibelly brought all her blankies from her room and tucked them in with ours. Then she added ribbons. Ribbons! In *my* room!

"Birds use ribbons in their nests," said Calvin, who always has a good word for Anibelly.

"Chirp, chirp," said Anibelly. "Nests have to be pretty."

That's the problem with having a girl for a sister. She can really ruin your style.

Then we filled a bunch of hot water bottles and put them in the nest to make it warm and cozy.

Then we climbed in, even Lucy.

Our nest felt like a warm bread basket.

"It's really nice in here," I said.

"Mmmm," said Calvin.

"I wouldn't mind being born here," I said.

Calvin was very quiet.

"If you move over a little," I said, giving Calvin a shove, "there'll be room for the baby."

Calvin shifted.

"No tossed baby green salad here," I said, pulling the covers closer.

"Zzzzzzzz," Calvin snored. "Zzzzzzzzzzzz."

Calvin was fast asleep.

And so was Anibelly on my other side.

And so was Lucy.

Usually, I'm up all night with my flashlight on account of all the monsters under my bed.

But not tonight.

Tonight, there was a space next to me for a baby. It was small and warm and quiet. It smelled like dreams. And it was shaped like me and Calvin and Anibelly and Lucy, put together like eggs in a nest.

Then I closed my eyes, just like that.

CHAPTER FIFTEEN

A Snow Day!

the house was quieter than usual the next morning.

I opened one eye.

Calvin was still asleep.

I opened the other eye.

Lucy was still asleep.

It sounded like the entire world was in stage three deep sleep, except for Anibelly, who's an early-bird special, and who was staring out the window, as still and frozen as the icicles on the other side.

It meant only one thing.

I popped out of bed and ran to the window.

"SNOW DAY!" I cried. "SNOWWWW DAYYYYY!"

"Rrrrfrrrfrrfrrrf!" Lucy barked.

"Hooray!" cried Calvin.

"Lalalalalala," Ani-belly began to sing. "Lalalalalala!"

It looked like sugar had spilled everywhere. I could hardly believe it!

After breakfast my mom bundled us in nineteen layers. Then we hurried outside.

There was nothing to do but roll around.

And scream.

And slide.

And dig tunnels.

And throw snowballs.

It was super-duper!

I'd been waiting FOREVER for a snow day.

Then I remembered that I'd also been waiting a long time to go to Scooter's house to see the baby. But there was never any time, until now.

"Don't stay long," my mom said at the door. "Hurry home, or your brother and sister will drink all the hot chocolate."

I squinted into the kitchen.

I saw the hot chocolate.

I smelled the hot chocolate.

I wanted the hot chocolate.

And Calvin and Anibelly were already drinking all of it!

But I also wanted to see the baby.

"Be right back!" I said. Then I turned and ran headfirst into the blinding light.

.●.●.

There was a big wooden bird in front of Scooter's house. It was a fancy sign that let people know that a brand-new baby had been dropped off at their house. "It's a boy!" the sign said.

I rang the doorbell.

"Hi!" said Scooter.

I said nothing.

"You wanna see the baby?"

I nodded.

"Okay," said Scooter. "Come in."

I went in.

"You have to be very quiet," Scooter said.

I was very quiet.

"You have to go through security," said Scooter. "Like at the airport."

Scooter waved a Jedi light saber over my body. "No firearms, poisons, choking hazards, pointy sticks, shampoo or electrical outlets allowed."

"Okay," I said.

"Take off your shoes," said Scooter.

I took off my shoes.

"And your snowsuit too."

"Why?"

"You can't go on a spy mission in a snowsuit," Scooter said. "The enemy will hear you coming."

I knew that. I peeled off my snowsuit.

"It's war," Scooter said, looking me smack in the eye. "We're in enemy territory and we need to find the enemy."

"What do we do once we find the enemy?" I asked.

"Spy," said Scooter.

I love spying. It's one of my talents.

First, we crept up the stairs.

Then we slithered down the hallway.

Then we cracked open the door to the enemy's hideout.

We crawled in undetected, even by the enemy's latest sonar listening device. . . .

Then we spied. . . .

The enemy was asleep like this:

We leaned in.

We spied some more.

Spying is really great! You notice stuff you normally don't see:

> The pearly shells of eyelids.
> Whispery hair.
> A head that breathes.
> Cheeks like sea glass.
> Cakepop fists.
> Fingernails like paper cutouts.

You stop breathing.

You stop moving.

You stop everything.

It was so quiet and still, you'd think we'd been kidnapped by a bunch of aliens or something and all that was left were our bodies, empty barnacles clinging to the side of a crib.

And maybe we had been kidnapped.

Not by a bunch of aliens.

But by one.

CHAPTER SIXTEEN

It's a . . .

i hurried home.

I could hardly wait for my mom to see the big wooden bird that I was dragging back with me. It was fantastic!

But first I had to stop by Flea's house to show it to her. She was making a snow volcano in her yard.

"Wow," she said. "You're stronger than you look."

I stood taller.

I panted like Lucy.

"That'll look great on your front lawn," Flea said.

I nodded.

"It's the perfect way to let people know that you're going to have a new baby brother," Flea said.

I nodded again.

Flea sighed. She stared at the sign. She didn't have any brothers or sisters. She was an only pirate.

I set the bird in her yard so that it looked like she was about to have a baby brother.

Flea smiled. She was very pleased.

Then we went to work on her snow volcano. It spewed snowballs! Then ice cubes! Then frozen, molten slush! It was super-duper!

After that I hauled my big wooden bird over to Jules's house, which is on the way to everything. Jules's mom was so impressed that she said I needed a cup of hot chocolate and cookies. Mmmm!

Then I made my way over to the cul-de-sac where everyone lives. First, I stopped at Sam's house, where there's always something to eat.

Then Nhia's house, where I had another snack.

Then Eli's house, where there's lots of candy.

Then Hobson's, where I was too full to touch anything, but Hobson's good at playing cards and so am I, so we played a few games of Go Fish, then War, then creepy Old Maid, and you can't play cards without getting the munchies, so I had a few pieces of his mom's famous home-made cake after all.

I didn't go to Pinky's house, but I pushed my humongous wooden bird slowly past it, just so he could see it from the street and feel jealous.

By the time I lugged it into my own yard, it was starting to get dark.

I could hardly wait to see my mom's face when she saw what I got for free!

"Mommmmm!" I cried, running into the kitchen.

Silence.

I grabbed a donut.

I looked around.

The house was shadowy and empty, except for Lucy, who came clicking across the kitchen floor.

"Where is everyone, Luce?"

"*Eeeee,*" Lucy whimpered. "*Eeee.*" Then she kissed me like crazy. And I kissed her back. If it weren't for Lucy, I'd have been all freaked out!

"Did my mom go to the hospital?"

Lucy blinked. She wagged her tail.

"Did she leave a note?"

I looked around again.

There was no purse.

There was no hot chocolate.

And—gasp!—there was no PDK!

The emergency Pregnancy Disaster Kit I had made for my mom was *gone*. And that's when I

KNEW SHE WAS IN THE HOSPITAL
HAVING HER BABY!!!

 Then I saw it—a lonely piece of paper on the
kitchen table:

Alvin --
 Gone to the hospital.
 Poh Poh will come get you.
 Don't worry.
            Love, Mom ♡

Gulp.

I didn't feel so good.

"Urrrrrgh," I moaned.

My belly turned square.

Then round.

Then irregular.

I felt like I was about to lay an egg!

Then I remembered what Calvin said: "Everything that happens to Mom will happen to you."

"Zounds!" I cried.

It was the worst bellyache I'd ever had!

"Ohhhhhh," I groaned. "What whalish, squiggly-bellied cankerblossom is this?"

I doubled over. *"Urrrrrrrrrh,"* I moaned.

Then I ran upstairs.

I needed to get to my birthing nest *fast*!

But first, I made a detour to the bathroom. My mom always says, when your stomach hurts, go to the bathroom.

So I did.

I looked out the window next to the toilet.

I looked at the calm, peaceful snow and the cheerful snowman that I had made with Calvin and Anibelly, and the big wooden bird that said, "It's a boy!" lying in the moonlit sugar.

I felt better.

But not for long.

Coming up the driveway, in the dark, I could just make out—gasp!—a man dressed in black. Carrying a black bag. It was the exact description of the thief on TV!

I flushed.

I wished I could flush myself away!

But I couldn't.

Worse, it was too late to reset Calvin's Rob Goldthug trap.

Loud, heavy footsteps came into our house, just. like. that.

Oops. I'd forgotten to lock the door!

I WAS NO LONGER HOME ALONE.

Gulp.

Quick, I darted into my room and dove into my closet.

And shut the door.

It wasn't supposed to happen this way.

My life wasn't supposed to end like this.

I had more scary stories to tell.

And more mochi cakes to eat.

And more tests to fail.

I was supposed to be around to meet my new baby brother.

And feel jealous.

And show him off.

And spy on him every chance I got.

I was supposed to turn out okay, like my dad, even though I was a lot of trouble now.

I was supposed to die an old man.

I pushed myself as far back into the closet as I could. I didn't want my body falling forward like a piece of cake when the shooting started. I wanted it to slump against the wall like a man.

I reached into the laundry.

I suited up.

That's the thing about death. It's important to go out in style, or it looks like you're just going to dig holes in your yard.

Then I landed on something hard.

My butt lit up.

It was Calvin's phone!

I pressed some buttons.

"Nine-one-one operator," said a voice. "Please state your emergency."

Thud. Thud. Thud. Thud. Footsteps came up the stairs.

"What is the nature of your emergency?" asked the phone.

Even if my voice had been working, I couldn't have said. The footsteps were in my room now!

I went headless.

But not before slipping the phone into the dirty laundry next to me to muffle the sound. The 911 operator can trace your call, as everyone knows, if you don't hang up.

I listened.

The wire tripped.

The fan turned on.

Calvin had set it!

The choo-choo train sped past the books.

Marbles clattered to the floor.

"AAAAAAAAAAAIIIEEE!" Someone was rolling on the marbles!

Then *THUUUUD!*

Silence.

Then I heard muffled sounds, like someone swearing into a pillow.

Oh no! The thief fell into our birthing nest!

NOT MY MOM'S BIRTHING NEST!!!

I breathed in.

I breathed out.

I burst out of the closet with my hockey stick.

Mushroom Mite to the rescue!

Then everything happened in slo-mo, like it does on the science channel right before Mount Vesuvius explodes and everyone dies.

There was hardly any light left in my

room, and I could just make out that the black figure was still facedown in the nest, struggling to get up, so I swung my hockey stick—

CRAAAAAAAAAACK!

And he went down again.

THUUUUD!

"Owww!" said the burglar.

I froze.

Oops.

It was supposed to be sudden death.

Now I was the one about to die!

He cursed. . . .

"What horrid, pinny-boned fish pizzle was that?"

GASP!

It was my dad!

"DAAAAD!" I wanted to scream.

But my teeth were all stuck together.

My dad looked dazed.

Then the blankets swallowed him like quicksand.

And I dove in after him.

Then I felt my dad's strong arms wrap around me, holding me tight.

"It's all right, son," he said, wiping blood from his nose. "You were defending your home."

I shook like tofu.

"I'd p-p-played hockey once m-m-myself . . . ," my dad stammered. "It's a great g-g-game. . . .

"You l-l-learn to get up and k-k-keep skating."

My dad squeezed me closer.

Then my dad explained that my mom had called him earlier when her labor pains started, and he'd rushed home.

"Lay-ror rains?" I mumbled.

"That's when your stomach hurts so much from trying to squeeze the baby out," my dad said.

I blinked.

I was having labor pains too!

"*Waaaaaaaaaaaaaaaaaaaaaaaaah!*" I cried. My mouth guard fell out.

My dad pulled me even closer.

I breathed him in.

I heard his heart.

I smelled his skin.

I was so glad my dad was home.

Then the cops came spinning up our driveway.

Wow. A cop car in our driveway. In the snow.

It was a terrific end to a terrifying week.

And it was the perfect way to rush me to the hospital to deliver my baby!

.•.•.

How to Ride to the Hospital
in the Back of a Cop Car
1. Look pregnant.
2. Look super-duper pregnant.
3. Look ready to burst!
4. Look like a criminal
   (easier than it sounds!).

At the hospital, we stopped at the window where the babies were sleeping like mummies all in a row, and breathed heavily.

After that, we went down the hall.

Then we stopped dead in our tracks.

There in a room was my mom and everyone else . . . and in her arms was the teeniest baby I had ever seen.

It was the size of a chinstrap penguin!

My dad and I floated toward it, like two astronauts in space.

I leaned close.

I breathed in.

I breathed out.

I breathed in the baby.

It glowed like a star.

And smelled like a kiss.

Then it opened its tiny mouth and yawned.

I was a "14.0, Nonfunctioning."

"Alvin," said my mom. "Meet your new baby sister."

My new baby whaaaaaaaaaat?

"Her name is Claire," said Anibelly.

"Isn't she cute?" Calvin asked.

Cute?

Lucky for me, there was another chance for a baby brother.

"When is *my* baby coming?" I asked.

"*Your* baby?" My mom looked puzzled.

"I'm eight months pregnant, aren't I? You said I have all the symptoms. Even your doctor said I was pregnant."

"A *sympathetic* pregnancy!" said my mom. "There's no baby in a sympathetic pregnancy."

"No baby?" It was not good news.

"You mean I got fat for nothing???"

Alvin Ho's
Simply Pathetic Glossary

American Revolutionary War— Started at North Bridge. The Redcoats said the bridge belonged to them and wouldn't let the Minutemen use it. There were bad words, then a gunshot, then more gunshots, then a bunch of dead bodies. Before anyone knew it, the war had started! It lasted from 1775 to 1783. In the end, someone had to build a new North Bridge.

Battle of Bunker Hill— Happened early in the American Revolutionary War (see above), but it wasn't on Bunker Hill. Low on ammunition, colonial soldiers were told, "Don't shoot until you see the whites of their eyes," which meant you should hold your fire until the enemy got close enough so you wouldn't waste your bullets.

Battle Road Trail— A five-and-a-half-mile path for biking, walking, running and wheelchairing that runs through Lexington, Lincoln and Concord. Paul Revere's famous midnight bike ride took place here.

cha-siu-bau— Means "barbeque pork packet" in Chinese. A round meat-filled bun made of flour and yeast, it can be steamed or baked. Very yummy!

Claire— My baby sister. She was supposed to be a boy!!!

Connecticut— (1) Mark Twain lived here, (2) his next-door neighbor was Harriet Beecher Stowe, (3) you can take tours of their creepy houses in Hartford, (4) south of Massachusetts, which is hard to spell, (5) even harder to spell than Massachusetts.

Dewey decimal system— A mysterious sequence of numbers used by aliens to organize all library books for transport into outer space.

dim sum— (1) means "dot the heart" in Chinese, (2) eaten for breakfast or lunch, little morsels of food, like shrimp balls or dumplings, that feel like you're putting polka dots on your heart, (3) tastes like happiness.

Dynamite Duo– Firecracker Man and Lucy!

Embarrassment Syndrome– A fatal condition usually caused by a girl. Symptoms include dry mouth, racing heartbeat, sweating, blinking, itching, confusion, memory loss, blurred vision and foot growth.

gestate– To carry something important inside you, like a baby or an idea.

Godzilla– A skyscraper-sized, radioactively mutated lizard.

Grocery Getter– A car used for getting groceries, and for drag racing.

hung bau– Means "red packet" in Chinese. A red envelope containing money! You get them for birthdays, New Year's, Christmas, Valentine's Day, Patriot's Day, Easter, the Fourth of July, the first day of school and sometimes for no reason at all except for being extra nice to

GungGung and asking him about the good old days in China.

Haiti earthquake— Happened in 2010. One of the worst natural catastrophes in history. Many people died, many were injured and nearly two million were left homeless.

hobbits— The Little People (no taller than a tabletop, but with the courage and strength of ten men) who live in the lands of Middle Earth in books by J.R.R. Tolkien. Their feet are covered with curly brown hair, like the hair on their heads, with leathery soles, so hobbits don't need to wear shoes. Oh, would that those feet were mine!

life savings— All the money you've saved up for your whole entire life, so that you can buy something really fantastic, like hobbit feet!

Lost Report Card Disorder— A fatal condition usually caused by mysterious circumstances that can never be explained. Symptoms include no report card, no sign of a report card, no memory of a report card, no hint that a report card was coming home, and sometimes the worst symptom of all: no clue whatsoever as to what a report card is, as in "A report card? Is that Chinese?"

Mites— (1) the youngest hockey players, aged eight and under, (2) a bug smaller than a tick; most are microscopic.

mochi cakes— Sweet, chewy little round cakes made from rice flour and filled with red bean paste. My pohpoh makes them. I can eat a hundred of 'em! Yummy when fresh; hard when left out for several days. Make great hockey pucks after a week!

nor'easter— A powerful storm that happens on the East Coast of the United States when warm winds from the south swirl in one direction and cold winds from the north swirl in the opposite direction. When the warm air and cold air hit each other with hurricane force—WHAM!—you get tons of snow and rain and killer winds.

Paul Revere— Rode his bike at midnight from Boston to Lexington to warn people that the British were coming. He stopped at every house along the way! The British busted him at Lexington and took away his bike.

PDK— Originally a Personal Disaster Kit, but now a Pregnancy Disaster Kit.

pregnancy test— (1) Answer yes to one or more of Calvin's questions and you pass, (2) the only way to know for sure whether you're pregnant.

pregnant— If you're truly pregnant, you have a baby growing inside you. But if you're simply pathetic pregnant, see below.

Redcoats— British soldiers, aka "lobsters" and "bloody backs," but the nickname "lobster backs" was not used until the War of 1812.

Rube Goldberg device— An invention that does a simple task in the most complicated way possible. Named for Reuben Lucius Goldberg, who drew lots of cartoons showing these machines. They're super-duper!

simply pathetic pregnant— First you get all the symptoms of being pregnant. Then you pass the pregnancy test. Then you eat everything. Finally, when you're ready to have your baby, there's no baby. You're just fat! It's terrible! Like my mom said, "All of the suffering and none of the glory."

spandex— Stretchy fabric that fits like a second skin. Favorite outfits of superheroes, swimmers, runners and bikers are made of spandex.

squillion!— An unknowable large number, too large to write without an exclamation!

stinky tofu— Stinky like baby poop, but yummy like . . . like . . . well, after I mention baby poop, nothing is yummy.

Thoreau— Henry's last name. A famous author who was born in Concord and died here too. His headstone in Sleepy Hollow Cemetery says only "Henry." In the basement of the Concord Free Public Library you can hold his handwritten manuscripts if you ask nicely.

UFO— Unidentified Flying Object.

ultrasound machine— aka Alien Detection Machine. Uses sound waves to look at the UFO inside my mom's belly.

Unfinished Homework Syndrome— Not a fatal condition, but you'll wish it were! Symptoms include no homework, and no clue that you had homework. More severe symptoms may include a dog with indigestion, strange baby poop, or kidnappings involving aliens whose diets consist mainly of human homework.

William Shakespeare— A British dude who wrote lots of plays, poems, curses, everything. He wrote so much that he ran out of words and had to invent nearly two thousand new ones. His invented words include: "amazement," "bump," "critic," "dwindle," "eyeball," "frugal," "gloomy," "hurry," "lonely," "majestic," "road" and "suspicious"!

Lenore Look is the author of the popular Alvin Ho series, as well as the Ruby Lu series. She has also written several acclaimed picture books, including *Henry's First-Moon Birthday, Uncle Peter's Amazing Chinese Wedding,* and *Polka Dot Penguin Pottery.* Lenore lives in Hoboken, New Jersey.

LeUyen Pham is the illustrator of the Alvin Ho series, as well as *The Best Birthday Party Ever* by Jennifer LaRue Huget; *Grace for President* by Kelly DiPucchio, a *New York Times* bestseller; and the Freckleface Strawberry series by Julianne Moore. She is the author and illustrator of the picture books *Big Sister, Little Sister* and *All the Things I Love About You.* LeUyen lives in San Francisco. Learn more at leuyenpham.com.

Afraid you've missed one of the Alvin Ho books?
Fear no more!

Alvin Ho: Allergic to Girls, School, and Other Scary Things

Alvin Ho: Allergic to Camping, Hiking, and Other Natural Disasters

Alvin Ho: Allergic to Birthday Parties, Science Projects, and Other Man-Made Catastrophes

Alvin Ho: Allergic to Dead Bodies, Funerals, and Other Fatal Circumstances

Alvin Ho: Allergic to Babies, Burglars, and Other Bumps in the Night